Reaching
for the Reins

To Pat & Shorty For Help A Kid Reach For Tha Reins —

Lou Dean

Lou 4/07

CLINESCOT
PUBLISHING
COLORADO

Thanks to Dr. L. L. and Jan Merrifield for inviting me to stay in the little house on the Arkansas River in the winter of 2000.

Thanks to a horse named, Dan, who first introduced me to the joy of swimming.

Thanks to Mary and Wally Finley, Mom and Ruth for their faith.

Thanks to the 'girlfriends' who believed in me enough to give this project wings.

Thanks to Jannis and Bill for their enduring support, to Jo Anne for the critter-care, and Jeanette for time.

Thanks to the Rangely Public Library

Thanks to Cecil Lollar

Back cover photo by Robert N. Nelson
Edited by Barbara P. Baker
Cover art by Jil Hegwer

For information or to order books call: 1-800-521-9221

Library of Congress Catalog Card Number: 00-93274

CLINESCOT
PUBLISHING
COLORADO

Blue Mountain Road, Dinosaur, Colorado

Printed in the United States

10 9 8 7 6 5 4 3 2 1

ISBN 0-9671208-3-7

To

Robert Scott Cline

The joy of your childhood was shadowed
by divorce
And you were tormented by the
school bullies
While fighting the demons of asthma
and dyslexia.

Because you conquered every challenge,
you now see
With the eyes in your heart.

I

Grief choked me as I entered the church and slipped unnoticed into a back pew. Parents sobbed and kids clung to each other with horrid expressions of shock shining in their blood-shot eyes. A song about love played in the background and I struggled to hear the lyrics, hoping the words would calm my storm of emotions.

As I watched the pastor comforting people I wondered how I'd gotten into the church. I had an eerie feeling that time had moved somehow forward and this was a memorial service. But, no, that wasn't possible, was it? The shooting had taken place just hours before. Hadn't it?

Lost in the midst of the confusion, I couldn't quiet my hammering heart. Here I was, among all the people whose lives had been changed forever. And no one knew my terrible secret.

Jacob never talked to me at school. I hadn't been seen with him anywhere. It was his way of protecting me.

"It's for your good, CJ. They hate me. Our friendship must be secret," he had said, in the Indian dialect he liked to practice. "No reason for parents to know. Don't talk to me at school or on the bus. Safer that way."

I shook as I sat and held myself with my arms.

Ten kids were lying dead in the halls of Fremont High as these people wept and prayed. Bodies that wouldn't be retrieved until the police could go over the crime scene. And poor Jacob. Everyone said he was crumpled over somewhere in the gym, near the boys he'd shot. But it couldn't be true. I tried to picture him alive with that 'doesn't matter' expression still on his face.

"Tokhe shni," he always said. 'It doesn't matter.' Tokhe shni. A hard knot throbbed in my throat.

Somehow, I'd convince people of Jacob's kind heart, his intelligence, how hard he tried.

My thoughts jumped to the present when a middle-aged woman slumped to the floor in front of the altar and several people circled around to comfort her. She sang "my son, my son" in a squall that reminded me of Jacob's voice that first time I spotted him near the Arkansas River.

He was naked from the waist up and barefooted. He had wild berry juice streaked across his face like war paint. I watched him for a while from the brush, wondering if I should walk out. His lonesome voice sang out a song of things so deep and hurting that it caused an ache in my heart.

Now I heard that hurt in some lady's voice, someone I didn't even know. Had Jacob caused her pain? People were calling him a lunatic coward. If Jacob was gone, I was the only one in the church who cared.

My mind leaped backward to earlier that afternoon. I stood and looked toward the school, with the damp

Oklahoma wind on my face. My eyes searched frantically as kids ran from the building. Where was Jacob?

Then, in the chaos of SWAT teams and sirens and shrieks of terror, I heard one of the seniors sobbing to the sheriff, "I don't think he goes to school at Fremont. I've never seen him before . . . but he's . . . shooting people. Shooting them. He aimed his gun right at me, then turned and shot . . . the guy next to me . . . he had these feathers hanging from his hair and his face was painted."

For the longest time I stood stone still. I couldn't move or speak. I just stood as the chaos banged and shrieked around me. *"I don't think he goes to school at Fremont."*

"CJ, we are invisible to these snobs."

"He had these feathers hanging from his hair and his face was painted."

"When I go down, CJ, I'll go as a warrior."

My knees gave out and I slumped to the ground. A young policeman ushered me off the school grounds yelling words that I couldn't hear above the screaming sirens. He led me to the end of the block, where crowds had started to gather.

That's when I heard. One of the nearby cop cars had the door open and the policeman was on his radio. "We have a name. Jacob Johnson. J A C O B J O H N S O N. Contact his family immediately and try to get them down here."

As parents started to arrive, they ran around searching for their kids, and screamed in relief or disbelief. I expected Jacob's Mom to emerge from the throng with her insolent friend, Drake, strutting by her side. I whispered

3

into the wind, "I wonder if they'll be sorry now, Jacob?"

Mrs. Johnson and Drake didn't know me, but I'd watched them from a distance, hiding, the way Jacob always wanted it. I'd seen a lot that they didn't know I'd seen.

I knew my mom wouldn't show and I was glad. She was off on one of her business trips. Probably cruising along the Cimmaron Turnpike between Tulsa and Stillwater, listening to a motivational tape.

For once, I was thankful to be alone.

Slowly, I realized I was still in the church. Again, I wondered how I'd gotten there. Had I heard the music and the people grieving as I walked by? Why were these other people here? Was this the closest church to the school? Had everyone else stumbled in looking for some way to make sense of things?

I looked at my watch. Five o'clock. I sat and tried to piece together the series of events that took place that afternoon. I was in study-hall. It must have been around 2 p.m.

Remorse draped over my shoulders like a damp shawl. But I couldn't cry. Everyone else was bawling. What was wrong with me? I was the only one in the room with dry eyes. I jumped up and stumbled outside.

I wandered back toward the school, but, by then, it was impossible to get within a block of Fremont High. Flashing lights sent up an eerie glow in the late afternoon light. Wails of grief echoed from the crowds of people who gathered, waiting, praying, hoping.

I turned and ran as fast as I could toward home. Fumbling with the key, I opened our apartment door and sat for awhile trying to blot out the horror.

Then it came to me. I had something I needed to do. I had to go to the river and get Prophet, Jacob's dog. I was the only one who knew about Prophet or Jacob's hideout. I jumped from the recliner and ran to the kitchen.

The answering machine blinked wildly. I stared at it for a moment. I didn't want to hear the messages. I knew my parents so well, I could hear both of their voices in my mind.

"CJ, call me immediately on the cell phone." Mom's crisp tone snapped in my imagination.

Then my dad's slow drawl crawled across the line all the way from Dallas, *"Connie Jean, honey, are you OK? I just heard about the shooting. Please call."*

I can't talk about it to anyone right now.

But I couldn't let them live in fear the next few hours. I pushed the OGM button on the answering machine and began to record. "I'm home, I'm . . . " I deleted the message and started again. "It's 6 p.m. the day of . . . the shooting. I'm OK, Mom, Dad. I've gone for a walk."

I grabbed some lunch meat, slipped on my jean jacket and hurried out the door.

Jacob's Border collie, Prophet, sat near the tee-pee, a forlorn look in his loving eyes. Jacob always came to him right after school. He never missed a day. The Arkansas River and the makeshift tee-pee were Jacob's security. He only went to his 'mama's house' when he had to change clothes to go to school. He never referred to it as home, always 'mama's house.'

Prophet didn't understand. He had no idea that his friend was gone forever. Jacob would never again sleep

5

with Prophet in his arms, walk along the river exploring with him, or teach him new words.

"Come 'ere, buddy. I'll take care of you. You will be my dog now." I took the bologna out of the package and fed it to Prophet, one slice at a time. He accepted the meat with quiet manners, licked the package, then nuzzled up under my hand in thanks.

The ache in my throat grew into a throbbing fist. I walked toward the river, stretching myself up straight and proud like Jacob used to do. I watched the new moon rise across the Arkansas River and tried to breathe deeply, but the breath couldn't slide past the lump in my throat.

Prophet walked up to me, scratched my leg and whined. His eyes looked worried. He sensed something was wrong.

"They said at the church, school will be out for the rest of the week," I told the dog. "I'll be back to visit you at first light. I'll come every day, just like Jacob did." Saying the words brought a trace of enthusiasm to my sick heart. Taking care of Prophet was my responsibility now. I focused on that and it helped, but only for a moment.

An image of Jacob came into my mind: his narrow, crooked nose and hawk shaped face, the lean body and thin frame that earned him the nickname, 'Bones' among the jocks at Fremont High. He loathed the name. Loathed the boys who gave it.

I kicked the base of a giant cottonwood tree and cursed. "You never even knew him," I said. "Never gave him a chance. He wasn't weak. He was stronger than any of you will ever be."

I thought about the day just a couple of weeks before

when I'd baked Jacob's favorite, chocolate chip cookies. I wrapped them in foil and started down to his spot near the river.

When I walked up, I put my hands together and whistled the call of the mourning dove, just the way Jacob taught me. "Awooo-woo-woo-woo." I was real proud that I did it right. After all those months, I still couldn't get it every time. But on that Tuesday afternoon, I sounded so good I half expected a lonely mourning dove to answer me.

Usually, Jacob took his own good time to return the call, which meant I could enter his little domain. He seldom did anything in a hurry.

That day, when he didn't answer or make any move to stand, I wondered what he was doing. I called again, "awoo-woo-woo-woo."

He sat Indian still, as only Jacob could. Sometimes it wasn't so hard to envision him as a warrior, even with his green eyes and sandy brown hair.

That was Jacob's fantasy, to be a renegade Indian riding free and wild on the plains. The father he had never known was some small part Sioux. Or so his mother said.

"One sixteenth," Jacob told me proudly one day, as if he were saying, "I am full blood Sioux".

Jacob read constantly about the Sioux tribe. 'My People' he called them. Sometimes he spoke in sign language and said Indian sounding words. I never knew for sure if they were real words or something from his imagination. He had Indian rituals that he took real serious. If he was in one of his 'meditations' I wasn't supposed to disturb him.

But he never got that mad at me or stayed mad very long, so that day, as I stood and waited with my chocolate chip cookies, I decided to chance it while the cookies were still warm.

When I stood in front of him and looked down, my heart sank. Even before he lifted his face, I knew. His eyes finally met mine and he said, "Sit".

I sat cross-legged facing him and put the paper plate of cookies between us. His lip was split and he had a shiner on his right eye.

"Your mother's boyfriend or the guys at school?" I asked. After a few minutes of silence, I began to get nervous and shoved the cookies toward him. "They're still warm."

He finally removed the foil, took a cookie and popped the entire thing in his mouth, munching. I knew it had to hurt his lip, because he winced.

I wanted to get Jacob's mind off his pain. "I read this book," I said, licking chocolate from my fingers. "Just finished it. It was about this guy who claims he can connect with the dead."

I knew Jacob pretty well by then. Knew he was embarrassed. Knew he was in pain and wouldn't talk about it. So l went on and on about the book, while he munched those cookies.

"The book appeals to me because of my grandfather. I miss him so much." I kept talking, but Jacob remained quiet.

When the last crumb was gone, Jacob stood and walked to the edge of the river and washed the blood from his split lip with the muddy water.

"Some day I will ride free," he said.

"Are you OK?" I asked, following him.

He slid one hand across his neck in a cutting motion. It was sign language for 'Sioux'. I knew that meant the visit was over.

I walked off into the woods and stood for a long time. I ached to go back and talk about real stuff, to cry with him, hold him and tell him he should move out away from the abuse at home. But I couldn't find the courage so I turned and walked away.

The memory made me sink down cross-legged in the sand and take Prophet in my arms. "Prophet, this hasn't happened. Our Jacob hated violence. He . . . had so much tenderness in him. Remember that day we found you? All beat to a pulp with blood matted in your hair? Jacob fell down on his knees right there in that alley and began to cry."

Prophet wiggled closer into my embrace and whined, as if he remembered. "Jacob carried you here, washed you and brought salve to doctor you. Finding you seemed to give him a reason to get up in the mornings. Remember when he began to teach you things? How excited he was to show me your tricks? He said you were smarter than most people."

I stroked Prophet's black and white coat. He whined and the expression in his eyes said he understood everything.

"That's why he named you Prophet. Jacob swore you were sent as a gift from the gods to lead the people to 'see with the eyes in their hearts.' Jacob said he saw it in a vision."

I kept rubbing Prophet behind his ears as words rattled out of me. "Jacob loved you with his whole heart. He was so kind to me and . . . I loved him. I did."

Then the soft whisper of a familiar voice echoed in my mind. "CJ." I pictured Jacob beside me, reaching for my hand.

I gasped for air and the ragged breath caught in my throat and burned.

II

Mom was home when I walked into the apartment. She held me at arms length and looked at me.

"You're OK?" my mother asked, then fumbled with an embrace. Her attempted hug turned into an awkward pat on my arm. "I'll fix us some herbal and draw you a hot bath."

I agreed with a nod.

Closing the lid to the stool, Mom sat and handed me my tea. I slid down into the security of bubbles and sipped the warmth into me, hoping it would somehow soothe the cold hardness that had replaced the ache in my throat and settled around my shoulders like a cast iron brace.

"Do you want to talk about it?"

"No," I answered, thinking, *please, just this once, listen to me. I don't want to talk. I just want you to sit, be near, be quiet.*

"It's so . . . unbelievable. I can't quite get a grasp on it, can you? Did you know that . . . boy? The one who went off the deep end? Can you imagine how his folks are feeling?"

It was time to analyze, look for solutions. Losing control or showing emotion wasn't Maggie McGee's style.

At least she isn't demanding answers.

"It's all this violence on TV. And the movies and video games. And the availability of guns. Something has to be done. Someone needs to declare war on the entertainment industry and the NRA. That's the only thing that will stop the insanity."

I thumped the surface of the water sending little splashes toward my feet. I wanted to scream, "Hogwash, Mom! I watch movies, play video games, even own a gun. I'm mad as hell at you and Dad and life and God, but I wouldn't shoot anyone and neither did Jacob." But I stopped myself just in time.

I let out a grateful sigh when the doorbell rang. Mom left the bathroom, then soon stuck her head back in. "William is here to . . . support us and your dad called. He's on his way."

Wonderful, I thought. *Mom's millionaire boyfriend. Dad and his new wife would soon arrive. My 'family' to the rescue.* I kicked my feet like a little kid throwing a tantrum. Water splashed out over the edge of the tub onto the floor, but I didn't care.

The old hurting sickness for home inflated my chest like a balloon. It had been a long time since I'd ached for things to be the way they had been, before the divorce. But sitting, sinking deeper and deeper into the tub of bubbles, I wanted only my mother and father. Wanted them to get along. Wanted the three of us to be a real family again. I let the fantasy play in my mind for awhile, until it turned as cold as the bath water.

I sat and waited for Dad to arrive. Mom and William cuddled on the couch and tried to get me to join them, but I chose the isolation of the recliner. The TV blared all the awful details, showing the scene of us kids running from the school. I stared at the screen in a kind of trance, only half-listening.

I seemed somehow removed from it all, as if it were just another night after homework before bed and I was watching another school shooting in some town in Mississippi or Oregon or Arkansas, thinking, *those poor kids.*

But the difference was the knot in my throat, the queasy nervousness in my gut and my trembling hands.

"Connie Jean." Dad came in the door like a blast without bothering to ring the bell. He grabbed me and held me in his vice-like arms. For a moment, basking in the security, I thought I would explode, shatter like an icicle falling from the eave of a house onto a sidewalk. I was thankful when he pushed me away just long enough to look into my eyes, to smooth a few strands of unruly strawberry hair from my face. The distance allowed me to swallow the grief that hung in my throat before it destroyed me.

When Dad released me his young wife, Cindy, gathered me into her arms with a dramatic little sob. I didn't resist the hug from my new stepmother, but quickly retreated. I wilted back into the recliner and Dad pulled a footstool up, sat right beside me and reached for my hand.

"I'm glad you're here," I said.

He nodded, holding my hand to his cheek. Cindy finally

ambled toward the couch, plopping next to William who was old enough to be her grandfather.

"William," Mom said, standing, "this is Alan, CJ's father and his . . . wife, Cindy." Then, looking right at Dad, she said, "This isn't your house. You knock next time."

"Here we go," I thought.

Dad looked sharply at Mom but didn't reply.

Filling the silence that followed, the national late newscasters talked about the most recent details on the school shooting. Mom clicked the remote volume up.

"And in this quiet suburb of Tulsa, Oklahoma, surrounded by wheat farms and cattle, tragedy today. The death count has risen to eleven, with six other students on the critical list. The shooter, seventeen year old, Jacob Johnson is reported to have turned the gun on himself after the shooting rampage. In a late-breaking development, the boy's mother is said to have given a statement to our NBC news affiliate. "We loved Jacob dearly and we don't understand any of this."

"I can't even imagine how those people must feel right now," Mom said.

The words triggered an image of Mrs. Johnson in my mind: back-combed red hair, heavy make-up and the ever present smell of beer and cigarette smoke on her clothes. Drake, her banty-rooster friend, front teeth missing, strutting beside her.

"We loved Jacob dearly."

The words sent a shock wave of rage vibrating down my back.

I'd seen Jacob's mother plenty of times, but she had

never seen me. Once I was actually in her house watching a documentary about the Plains Indians with Jacob when Mrs. Johnson and her boyfriend, Drake, came home. Jacob hid me in the closet.

I stood, rigid with fear, listening to Drake's raspy, impatient voice as he attacked Jacob. "Get your ass up here and wash that damned war paint off your face. You're as worthless as your bum father. For Christ sake, why don't you grow up."

In the closet, trembling with fear, I waited for Jacob's mother to defend her son, waited for her to tell Drake to shut up, but she didn't say one word. Then I heard a thud against the wall and heard Jacob moan. I visualized Drake with his shirt stretched tight over his beer belly, his rough hands coming down hard across the back of Jacob's thin shoulders. The image made me cringe deeper into the closet.

Then, as if nothing had happened, Jacob's mother began to talk about her shift at the tavern that day.

Barely breathing, I knew for the first time what Jacob's life was really like, day after miserable day. I could smell the stench of old beer and cigarette smoke on his mother when she came to the bedroom to get a jacket. I heard the hacking, wheezing lungs struggle for air in between drags on the cigarette. Even from the closet, the smell burned my throat and I held my hand over my mouth to keep from choking.

When Mrs. Johnson and Drake finally left a couple of hours later to make a 'beer run', Jacob came to me. He looked so humiliated when he opened the closet door.

I fell into his arms bawling and he held me awkwardly just for a moment, then ushered me quickly out the back and toward the river. Sitting cross-legged in the security of his tee-pee, I cried while he sang out his Indian song of pain. And I knew that, although Jacob openly hated Drake, part of his anger had to be toward the mother who stood silently by and allowed the abuse.

"Honey, are you OK?" My father's voice echoed somewhere in the far distance. "Connie Jean, maybe you should try to get some rest, sweetheart."

I nodded and looked at my father. In a weird daze, I stared at the foreign images in the room; William, with his walnut sized opal ring, then Cindy, fidgeting with impatience. I zapped William and Cindy off the couch, then put my Dad next to Mom. In a world of chaos, family was something that should stay forever the same.

"Have fun," I said, and walked toward my bedroom. I knew the arguing would start the minute I walked from the room. One more battle in the five-year war.

III

Sleep came with disturbing images as I fought the covers and moaned. I opened my eyes and lay in panic. Had I heard gun shots?

For several moments, I lay frozen with fear. The sound of Mom taking a shower, the muffled radio, and a gentle swish of limbs blowing outside my open window began to quiet my heart.

Memories rolled across my mind like a garbage truck banging down an alley. Gun shots, screams, blood, disbelief. Then an image of Jacob, slumped over, lifeless.

I flopped onto my belly and buried my face in the pillow, but the memories kept coming, getting closer, louder in my mind. The garbage truck was right behind me and threatening to run me down. I squeezed my head between my hands until the pressure made the thoughts stop reeling.

Then I thought of Prophet. He needed me. I jumped out of bed, dressed quickly and sneaked out without telling Mom.

I scribbled a quick note and propped it up between the crystal salt and pepper shakers on the dining room table. Dad would be calling from his motel and if I had disappeared, he'd worry.

"GONE FOR A WALK, BACK SOON . . . CJ" I left the time off on purpose, because I didn't want to return. Didn't want to watch TV or look at a paper or go around the school. Didn't want my parents trying to get me to talk about it. Maybe if I blocked it all out, the distance would erase some of the memory.

I was thankful for all the walks I'd taken over the last few months. I had told Mom I might try out for track. It was a lie. I was spending the time with Jacob, but I knew she was relieved because I wasn't interfering with her schedule.

I stopped at the corner store and paid the clerk for a small sack of dog food. The man was talking to the bag boy about the school shooting.

"It's totally unbelievable. Too bad that kid shot himself. He deserved to be hanged."

"You didn't know him!" I wanted to scream. I grabbed my sack and stumbled out of the store. Just outside, Jacob's face stared up at me through the bars of the newspaper rack. The top half of the front page showed Jacob's picture with the words, MASSACRE, beneath it. I began to run, the knot crawled back into my throat, like an iron fist choking me.

Prophet met me with an enthusiastic bark, but then sat down and looked past me, as if he expected Jacob. I walked on and called him. "Come." He responded obediently, just as if he were minding Jacob. "Lie down," I said, and he promptly went to the ground, putting his head on his paws and looking up at me.

I thought of all the days Jacob spent training his dog. *In some small way, maybe it will comfort Prophet.* "Heel," I said. I walked through the trees as fast as I could, crashing through the underbrush and dodging limbs the way Jacob used to do. When I turned, Prophet walked just behind my left leg.

"Good boy," I said. I knelt and allowed him to eat his fill of dog food from the sack, then took him in my arms. He whined and looked around, his eyes confused and tormented. The look sliced at my heart.

"Come," I said, then turned and started back. I stood for a long time and stared at Jacob's tee-pee. His labor of love. He'd hand-cut each of the six straight, strong poles from young cottonwood trees and bound them at the top with leather thongs.

He then wrapped the structure with an old army tarp that he referred to as his buffalo hide. With a small stick fire, the lodge could be made toasty, even in the windy months of winter.

I'd only been invited into the lodge on one occasion, the day after Jacob hid me in his closet. After his mother and Drake had left the house, I started shaking all over and bawling. Jacob led me down to the river and into his lodge. He quietly built a fire and brewed some sassafras tea from roots, offering it to me from a gourd cup.

The vivid memory made me stand and stare at the tee-pee. I had the urge to go in, but I couldn't. Jacob wasn't inside and the emptiness would swallow me. I turned and ran toward the apartment. Prophet followed me into the clearing. I stopped and looked at him through blurry eyes.

"Go back!" I screamed. He responded to the command, turning and slinking off. An ache started again in my throat as I walked away. I didn't want to leave him. I knew the landlord wouldn't allow him in our plush apartment and Mom wouldn't consider moving. But somehow I had to find a way. He needed me. And I knew . . . in the next few weeks I would grow to need him more and more. He was the only link left to Jacob.

I heard my father's angry voice and I stopped on the steps.

"If you hadn't moved her from Dallas. Made her give up her horse and dog and life . . . all her friends. She's never been happy since. Never been the old carefree Connie Jean. How can she ever be? Moving around with you every six months, every time your precious career in real estate jerks you to a new hot spot? She deserves to have a home, Maggie, where she can establish friends."

"Excuse me," Mom's voice was indignant. "You mean like the home she had before you started screwing around on me? Aren't you the bastard who left US? Was that fiasco of you and your . . . child boss just some fucking nightmare CJ and I went through by mistake?"

"That a girl, Maggie," Dad said, "refuse to take your part of the responsibility. It was all my fault, that's fine. We've been through all of that a hundred times before. I'm guilty, it's over. Now, can't we at least try to think of Connie Jean, of her best interest? Just this once? Can't you admit to yourself that THE most important thing in life is your career? Has always been your career? Connie Jean and I ran second always."

"Oh, here we go. Now it's time for you to tell me how I abandoned my own child by putting her in day care when she was only three so I could go back to work. How I should let her come live with you, so she can have a 'real' home where Mommy will be baking cookies every afternoon when she comes in from school. But then, the new Mrs. McGee can afford such luxuries, since her daddy owns the company, owns half of Dallas."

"You selfish little brat. It always comes back to money with you, doesn't it?"

"And money isn't important to you?"

I couldn't stand anymore. Bursting through the door, I stomped in and slouched in the chair.

Dad strolled over with a guilty look and reached for my hand. "Connie Jean, why don't you come down to Dallas with me and finish this semester? Get away from this mess, heal for a few weeks, then, if you'd like to stay . . . "

"You forget," Mom walked over and stood behind my chair like a lion guarding her cub, "I have custody of CJ."

"And that's more important than her well-being, Maggie? For God's sake."

"She's fifteen, she can decide for herself. If that's what she thinks is best, then I'll go along with it." Mom looked down at me. Dad squeezed my hand.

The only thing I thought about was Prophet. He needed me and I couldn't leave him. "I can't leave right now, Dad. But thanks for the offer."

"I hate it that you have to stay and go through all of this,

Baby." His voice was genuine and I knew he was concerned. More worried than my mom. Maggie loved me in her own detached way. But her attitude was more like, 'I gave you life, now live it. You don't need me, I'm busy.'

But I knew living at my father's wouldn't be easy. His top priority was Cindy and the fact that she was part of the entire messy equation still made me mad.

My father took a step toward the door. I stood and followed him. "I'll call you every day."

"That'll be great," I said, in a voice drained of enthusiasm.

"If you change your mind or just want to come down for a weekend, I'll buy you a plane ticket." He looked at me and his eyes filled. "All of your old friends, Matt and Kelly and Suze all still ask about you." My father struggled. Was he trying to say he was sorry that the divorce had screwed up my life? He fidgeted, but remained quiet.

"Tell them all I said, Hi," I said, thinking that my old world, my childhood home and life were more distant than he knew.

"I've talked to Cindy about buying another acreage out near our old home place. She's OK with that. You could have a horse again, get back into 4-H with your old friends. Come home."

You Don't Understand! I wanted to scream. *I can't come back now. It's not the same. I'm not the same.*

"New bait?" Mom said, her eyebrows raised.

"We could go back to court, you know. Circumstances have changed somewhat . . . in the last two years," Dad said.

I didn't have enough energy to listen to them start again.

"They're having memorial services today for some of the kids. I have to go, Dad. I didn't really even know them, but I have to go."

"I understand." Dad gave me another lingering hug and planted a kiss on my hair. "Please take care of yourself and call me if I can do anything."

I stood in the shower and let the hot water pelt down over my face and throbbing head. I thought about home. On the outskirts of Dallas, the small farm house nestled in the trees with a wide creek running behind.

For a few moments, I let soft memories flutter through my mind like tiny butterflies darting over clover. Warm, fuzzy, fleeting thoughts of friends giggling, sharing deep secrets in hidden places.

"The great thing about divorce," I said, with the water warming me, "parents get to start over with new lives, while the kids' childhoods lie in shattered pieces around their feet. Forever."

Then my thoughts traveled through the past five years. *Shock at the news of my parents' divorce announcement. Custody court battles. Good-byes. Tears. Anger. Then . . . Wichita. Life after Wichita, Kansas hadn't been worth living until I met Jacob.*

Disbelief was still the only reaction I had to the shooting. Jacob couldn't do such a thing. When the scene from Fremont began to replay in my mind, I let the water pelt me straight in the face. I turned the hot water off and the cold blast shocked my body and made me shiver.

At the breakfast table, Mom was eager to fall right

back into her schedule as if nothing had happened.

"Can I do anything?" she asked, as she buttered a piece of toast and handed it across the table. "I could cancel the things on my schedule." She said the words with a hint of hesitancy, like 'please say no'.

"It's OK, Mom. I'll be fine."

"What's on the agenda?"

"I'm going to attend some of the memorial services. I didn't know the boys, but I think I should go because of . . . "

Mom's eyebrows arched in question. "Because of ?"

"Because it's my school, you know." I'd almost said, 'Jacob. Because of Jacob.' In the silence that followed I thought about how shocked my mother would be if she knew that I was a good friend with the boy accused of the atrocity.

"Were you close to any of them?" Mom asked.

I gave a bitter chuckle. "Sure, Maggie, I'd been to parties with them, gone on double dates, talked about all the little intimate things that best friends talk about."

She looked at me, with raised eyebrows, "Getting smart with me won't help things."

As usual, Mom would avoid any of the problems I faced and focus on her career endeavors. She didn't want to talk about the fact that I hadn't had any real friends since Dallas because I'd changed schools every six months.

Sometimes I would try to bait her into discussions by being a smart ass, but more often than not, she wouldn't play the game.

Part of me wanted to shock her right out of her chair and onto the floor. *I knew the one accused of the Massacre,*

Mom. Knew him well. I loved him. I said it to her in my mind. I smeared peach butter on a piece of toast, sipped on hot tea, and thought about Fremont High. Dread settled over me. I was thankful in that moment I didn't have any friends. I thought about Suze back in Dallas, of Matt and Kelly. I visualized them on the floor in pools of blood, cold and ashen. I slowly put the uneaten toast back on the plate and tried a swallow of tea. The knot of pain in my throat didn't go down.

But I didn't know them because they wouldn't let me.

I fought hard for their friendship in the beginning. Fought to break through the little cliques. I joined every possible club, remained nice even when the girls were nasty. In time, my efforts at Fremont High faded, just like earlier attempts to make friends in previous schools.

Jacob and I talked some about being an outsider. He'd been alone since third grade, when the bigger boys began to chase him and pelt him with rocks after school. His sentence was handed out, not because of being the new kid, but because he was shy and wasn't athletic.

"At first, scared. Run home and hide. By seventh grade, I fought back. Couldn't beat them. Always too big. Too many. But then I could fight no longer," he said, his voice thick with emotion. "It hurt me inside." He thumped his hand over his heart with his fist.

I hadn't dealt with the physical pain or constant brutality. Girls had a different kind of torment. They called names, whispered and shut me out. But Jacob suffered more. When I ignored the girls, after awhile they stopped. Boys didn't stop.

Day after day, I watched from a distance while the jocks of Fremont High tripped Jacob, pushed him against the lockers, called him every low-life name imaginable, cursed and even spat on him. And many times, after Jacob and I became friends, I had to fight myself not to jump into the middle of his tormenters.

What are you doing? He's a person with feelings and goodness and love inside of him, just like you. Why are you being so mean?

"I'm off," Mom said. "Would you like to go out and have Italian tonight? It's Friday."

Spending money on me was Mom's way of trying to make things better in my life. Her efforts always intensified when I retreated from her. I'd grown more and more pissed because money seemed to be the driving force that made her get out of bed each morning.

"It doesn't matter," I said, and the words immediately echoed into my mind with Jacob's Indian dialect, *tokhe shni.*

"Well, if you need me today, call on the cell."

I nodded.

I sat and stared out the window. Raising it slightly, I let my mind become intoxicated with late spring. I listened to the Oklahoma wind blow, watched the blossoms on the red bud trees dance, and smelled the sweet iris that lined the sidewalk.

Jacob and I had planned to fish and explore the river as soon as school let out. He said we'd somehow get our hands on two horses and ride.

A few weeks ago Jacob revealed a special plan he had for us. "We will do a sweat together, then fast. For two days we will seek the mystical reality beyond the surface of our souls."

I walked into the living room and clicked on the remote. Jacob's face was plastered on the screen. "And so, the day after the horrific massacre, the death count is officially eleven, counting the shooter, Jacob Johnson. Most of those fatalities are young athletes. Reports are coming in to us that Jacob Johnson was sometimes picked on by the athletes. It appears that this mass murder-suicide was a pay back mission."

"Sometimes!" I shouted to the TV. "They never missed a day." But I immediately had regrets when I pictured the bodies of the strong young men lying dead.

"Today, after the tragedy, students and parents, family and friends are expected to attend five different memorial services being held this afternoon at neighborhood churches. In the meantime, our national leaders are looking for answers to school violence. The president will hold a press conference later this afternoon. Issues of TV violence and guns are expected to be the hot topics." The reporter seemed hungry to keep talking about the shooting.

"Why don't you talk about parents?" I asked, "About how they're screwing up their kids' lives? Why don't you talk about divorce and alcoholism and abandonment and stepparents and what it's like to be fifteen and hate life?" I screamed.

I jerked up my back pack, pulled out the spiral notebook and began to write as fast as I could. Words kept blaring from the TV, but I couldn't hear them. As usual, when I wrote, everything faded except the pen and paper in front of me. I could barely keep my hand moving fast enough to write my thoughts.

When the urgency began to slow and the blaze inside me dimmed to hot embers, I looked back up at the television. They showed the school as we all ran from the building the day before, hands over our heads. The chaotic scene spread out several blocks around the school in every direction, parents running toward the building in terror, screaming for their kids. Cops, firemen and SWAT team members were moving in frantic spurts, trying to help wounded kids, talking on cell phones. The kids clinging to each other and bawling. It looked like an anthill that had been splashed with gasoline and set on fire.

The mayor's face came on the screen. I clicked the volume back on.

"We've increased security at all of our inner city schools and the suburbs. It's time to get tougher with gun control."

The gun. For the first time, I remembered the gun. Jacob had shown it to me. It was some fancy automatic rifle Drake recently bought at a gun show. "It belongs to Drake. He likes guns. Likes to play little big man." Then aiming it at the river, he fired off a round at a water snake. He caught it just below its head and the snake flipped into two wiggling, bloody stumps.

The sight didn't bother me. I thought of my own pistol, a twenty-two that my grandfather bought me for that same exact purpose, shooting snakes. Poisonous snakes in Oklahoma were common. I learned early how to shoot them without regret.

"Jacob," I said, touching his arm. "Are you OK?"

"Tokhe shni," he said, then sank into his cross-legged

posture. "I wish I could live in yesterday," he said. "Ride free."

"He didn't do it," I whispered out loud. "He just couldn't have." I clicked the remote off and grabbed a jacket.

I stumbled toward the school grounds, making my way through masses of people.

Amazing Grace played softly in the distance as lines of mourners brought flowers to the school yard in memory of loved ones.

No one will bring flowers to honor you, Jacob. If I tried to, I would probably get lynched. You're left alone one final time. Always alone.

"I care about you, Jacob. They mean nothing to me. Not one of them was ever nice or cared one twit for either of us." But the memory of losing my grandparents, the pain of trying to say good-bye to someone I'd loved made me numb with guilt for saying the words.

Two arms reached out and caught me in an iron clasp.

"Oh, CJ, I've been worried about you. Hadn't seen you. Are you OK?"

It was the one person at Fremont High I cared about. "Mrs. Mac," I said, lingering for a moment in the chunky embrace. My English teacher was the type to never let anyone go unnoticed.

One day when Jacob and I discussed the snobs at Fremont High he challenged me to name one person who cared.

After a lot of thought I said, "Mrs. Mac."

A slow smile flickered around Jacob's mouth. He hated to admit it, but he knew I was right. Mrs. Mac was one person at Fremont High who made a point to love everyone.

"I'm OK, Mrs. Mac. I'm OK," I said, lingering in the bear hug.

The teacher pushed her glasses up from her nose and nervously straightened my jean jacket. She looked at me with that look that let you know you were not invisible.

"Poor Jacob," she said. I stared, surprised that even Mrs. Mac could have sympathy for Jacob after all of the accusations.

I'd written a lot of essays about my deepest secrets in Mrs. Mac's class. About my parents' divorce, how it wrecked my life. About selfish parents who cared only about acquiring things, while their kids went unnoticed. How life really sucked for kids because family was gone and all that was left was fear and insecurity. How things were changing so fast and we lived in this gray world where nothing was concrete. How dating was a confusing pressure game of sex and manipulation.

I knew all of my intimate thoughts were safe with Mrs. Mac. But I'd been careful not ever to mention Jacob's name. I honored Jacob's wish that not one person could ever know of our friendship.

"Come on," she said, grabbing my hand. "The first memorial service is at the Catholic church. I have my car and I need a buddy."

So for the next three hours, I stumbled into one church after another, watched the pain-stricken faces parade up in front of the pulpit placing flowers. I heard cries of anguish, disbelief, and shock. Smelled the sweetness of flowers until it nauseated me. The entire time, all I thought about was Jacob. There would not be a service that day for Jacob, Mrs. Mac said.

In a way, I was relieved. A part of me believed he was still alive. They had mistaken Jacob for someone else. Some stranger who sneaked into Fremont that day and committed the crime. Jacob would be back on the river that evening, waiting for me.

As I sat in the car listening to Mrs. Mac chatter, I knew she was trying to help me. She didn't know it, but nothing she could say would help.

"Are you going back to spend some time in Dallas with your Dad this summer?" Mrs. Mac made it a point to know every single detail of her students' private lives. On the first day she made us all write an essay on 'My life at home is . . . '

Then she told us, "I can't possibly love you unless I know you. I intend to love each and every one of you before this semester is over, whether you like it or not. It isn't optional. Start telling me about yourselves."

I liked her that first day. How can you not like someone who just comes right out and says, "I will love you no matter what. No matter how ugly you are, how stupid you are, how many mistakes you've made. I'm going to love you."

My teacher repeated the question when I didn't answer. "Are you going to your Dad's soon?"

I nodded. "It's set up that way in the . . . custody agreement. My dad gets me in the summer." It sounded so strange to say the words out loud, 'My dad gets me in the summer.'

31

Being in Mrs. Mac's class had helped me deal with some of the anger of my parents' divorce. When I began to write it down it clarified some of my confusion.

Once I wrote an essay on parents who divorce. I really let them have it. Talked about how selfish divorce was. How two people who made a conscious decision to have kids should have to stay together at least until the kids were adults. It should be a written commitment. Some legal, binding agreement they could get out of only because of extreme conditions of abuse. Even then, if the marriage had to end in divorce, the custodial parent was bound by the contract to continue her responsibility toward the child and not remarry until the kid was eighteen.

Mrs. Mac gave me an A+. She suggested I let my parents read it. I gave it to Mom and watched her expression when she started reading. She didn't finish it, but instead gave a short laugh.

"This is good writing, CJ. Your subject is . . . a little unrealistic, but the writing is good."

Her words really burned me. "Why is it unrealistic?" I asked.

"Because life just isn't that cut and dried."

"It used to be. Divorce used to be the exception, not the rule."

"There were a lot of miserable people too," Mom said.

"And today with the divorce rate 50% or more everyone is blissful, right? Especially the kids?"

"So you're saying that two people should stay together in spite of everything?" Mom had that 'you're so naive' tone in her voice.

"We have birth control. If two people make a conscious decision to have a kid they ought to also commit to stay in the marriage until the kid is an adult. The only exception being extreme cases of abuse or neglect. Then the remaining parent still has to commit to the kid and not put her career or personal life first until the kid graduates. They can't remarry or uproot their kids from the home they've always had."

Mom let out a short laugh of disbelief. At least she was talking. I took advantage of the opportunity to get it all said.

"Adults today are selfish. They want this and they want that. The perfect relationship, great sex, money, THINGS. They don't give a damn that in the process their kids are flopping around like fish on a creek bank. They just want what they want."

"You think I divorced your father because of some selfish pursuit?" Mom was pissed and it felt good for it to be her for a change, so I continued.

"I think you and Dad had problems, differences from the beginning. But you still chose to have me. I'm saying if people want to be parents they have to choose. Live with the adjustments of marriage, agree to compromise and sacrifice certain things until their child is grown, or don't become parents in the first place."

"Oh, CJ, you have so much to learn."

I smiled and threw my last stone. "Maybe God invented marriage so two people would actually have to learn to love each other unconditionally."

Mom shot me a killing glance, but the thought left her without words.

"Too big a concept for you, Maggie?"

"Go to your room this instant."

I smirked and strutted off, temporarily satisfied.

Thirty minutes later, Maggie McGee strolled into my space and invited me to the mall. I stared at her and wanted to lunge at her throat, knock her down and choke her until she gurgled.

Mrs. Mac asked me the next day if I'd let Mom read it.

"Yeah," I said, with a sarcastic grin.

"Didn't go too well, huh?"

"Let's just say we didn't agree."

"Maybe you could try with your Dad."

"Why bother?" I said. "Neither of them will stop pointing a finger at each other long enough to admit they screwed up my life."

When Mrs. Mac and I left the last church gathering, I knew I could never attend even one of the funerals. I'd never survive it. I got this vivid image of my lively grandfather in his casket all ashen and cold. I remembered how long that memory had haunted me.

"I think funerals are barbaric," I said. "When I die I want to be cremated and scattered on the wind. I sure don't want people staring down at my cold empty carcass."

Mrs. Mac stopped the car in front of my apartment and stared in silence for a moment. She seemed to be struggling with a response. "I know everyone is placing all the blame for this on Jacob," she said, looking right at me. "But I take responsibility for not trying harder to know him. I should have done more. I always felt he had a bad home situation and I know the kids picked on him. I tried talking to him, but he was such a quiet one." She seemed to be waiting for a response.

"He didn't do it," I said.

My teacher let out a little gasp. She reached quickly for my hand and patted it. "Oh dear, you're in shock. Like we all are. It's just so hard to believe."

"Thanks for being with me today. For the ride home," I said and reached for the car handle.

"Oh, you were with me, child. Thank you." A rare look of intensity crossed the wide brow. "Are you going to be OK? Is your mother home? Can I do anything at all?"

I looked at the love in the soft gray eyes behind the upside down glasses. Mrs. Mac often spoke in triple sentences.

"Thanks," I said, opening the car door.

"Let's take that fishing trip we've talked about. Summer's just around the corner. I haven't been in years."

I agreed with a nod, getting out of the car. As I walked up the sidewalk toward the apartment, Mrs. Mac shouted, "You keep writing, you hear? Write about it all. Get your feelings out."

The minute I walked in the door, I knew something was wrong. It wasn't even five o'clock and my mom was home. Her face was set in a determined frown and her blue eyes sparked and darted as she asked me to sit down.

"Your father," she said the word like a curse, "your father is taking me back to court to try to get permanent custody of you. Can you believe it?"

"I can believe damn near anything." I said the words before I stopped to think.

"Connie Jean!" My mother never called me by my full name. She'd been calling me CJ for fifteen years.

"I just don't care anymore, Mom. You and Dad are gonna do what you do. I'm just a pawn in your games of revenge."

My mother stared, wordless. She wrestled with a response, but apparently couldn't think of one. "You need some counseling. I know they've set up trauma centers around town and have counseling for all the kids at Fremont High."

I gave a short laugh. "Yeah, Mom, I need help."

"Well, do you want to go back to Dallas, live with your dad . . . and Cindy?"

Mom could have been a military genius. She was a master in the art of war. She knew Cindy was the one thing keeping me from that choice. She knew I missed Dallas. Missed having a horse, being with the country kids I grew up with. She knew that living in town and changing schools often wasn't a picnic, but then neither would Cindy be. I blamed Cindy in a lot of ways for the divorce. If Dad hadn't met her, if she hadn't been so willing to fall in love with him, hadn't given him the attention Mom wasn't giving . . .

"Actually, I'd love to live alone at this point. I'm sick of you both." I walked out the door while my mother was still talking.

Prophet met me with an eager whine. I took the remaining dog food from where I'd stashed it in the fork of the tree and opened the bag, folding it down. He sat beside me and munched the hard chow while I stroked his back.

"They're at it again," I said out loud to Prophet. "The great war rages on. Battle of the minds, battle of the courts, battle of the wills. And I'm the prize."

I rubbed Prophet's ears as he ate. "The irony of it is, I'm no longer a child and they don't even realize that. I lost all of my innocence . . . in Wichita."

For a moment I allowed myself to think back on that awful time in Wichita. The time when I went from a child to a young adult because of one stupid choice. How I yearned to confide in my parents but couldn't. How alone and scared I'd been until Mom and I moved to Tulsa and I met Jacob. The thought of being that alone again overwhelmed me with despair.

When Prophet finished eating, he walked a few steps away from me and barked. He wagged his tail and jumped, then bounced out and looked back.

"What is it, buddy? You want to walk?" I stood and began to follow him. He took me along the path by the river and led me up the hill toward the farm house. "Where are we going? Wait up."

As I walked up breathless toward the corral, I kept thinking, *why is Prophet leading me here?* But then I knew. It was part of his routine, something he was missing since Jacob left. Every single day for four months, Jacob had come and talked to the paint horse. The first day Jacob led me up, he wouldn't tell me what we were going to see.

"Just follow," he said, moving along the path and up the hill. When we stood looking at the gorgeous palomino paint, I remembered the change in his voice. "Someday I will ride free," he said. The words were soft and throaty, as if he were choked with emotion. "Someday I will ride free."

He pointed to the FOR SALE sign on the gate. "I will own him one day." He crawled between the boards of the holding pen and went to the pony.

I watched while he gently ran his long slender fingers over the paint's entire body. The pony trembled slightly beneath his touch then gave a soft blow of breath and turned to cradle his beautiful golden head in Jacob's arms.

Prophet gave a bark that jolted me back to the present. He looked at me, then squirmed under the fence into the corral. The horse put his nose down to the dog and the two of them seemed to exchange a great secret. Prophet barked again, jumping and twisting around the spotted pony.

"You want me to pet him?" I asked. The answer was an immediate, husky, 'woof.'

I stood, hesitating. I had never been in the corral with the horse. I'd always stood outside while Jacob touched and handled him. I wasn't afraid of any horse. I was afraid of myself. What it would do to me if I ever loved one again and had to give him up.

An image of Bandit came vividly to me. The bay gelding's keen eye and broad chest, his strength beneath me as we competed in the rodeos running the barrels. The way his keen agility and quiet power always gave me confidence. I remembered his warm breath against my hair, the way he'd nibble gently at the curls on my shoulder, careful not to pull too hard.

I shook off the memory. Bandit belonged to someone else now. Sold in an auction like an unloved mustang heading for the meat market. One more statistic in my parents' war.

Prophet barked at me. The pony took a step forward and gave an inviting nicker. "No," I said flatly and turned. I walked quickly back toward the river and Jacob's retreat.

I held Prophet for a long while at the water's edge and tried to meditate the way Jacob had taught me. Breathing in through my nose and puffing the breath out of my mouth. Imagining an arrow of soft light coming into my body, traveling gently up and around then going out. I kept seeing Bandit, feeling him beneath me. The two of us were flying in the wind, running free along the banks of a great muddy river. There was a black and white dog with us and we were getting away. Away from the fear and the anger and the sadness.

"Someday I'll ride free." Jacob's voice was so real, it jarred my eyes wide open.

"I have to go, Prophet," I said, getting up and starting toward town. He followed me but didn't turn back where he usually did. I stopped on the path and pointed toward the river. "Go back," I scolded.

Prophet hit the ground, putting his head on his paws.

"No. Go back, Prophet," I said, trying to lower my voice to sound more like Jacob. "You can't follow me."

Prophet took several crawling steps, inching his way toward me and whining. I looked around for something to throw. I picked up a small stick, but the look on his face made me drop it immediately. I thought of my Australian Shepherd, Twain. The fear in his eyes that day I'd left him with a neighbor. The day I'd left Dallas to go with my mom.

I walked to Prophet and knelt down. He worked his way up into my lap, putting his head against my neck. Thinking about Twain, about leaving him, put a familiar twist of anger back in my stomach. The anger slithered around until it found a safe place, then it lowered its head. "I'll find a way to take you," I promised. "I'll find a way. But for now, you have to go back and wait for me."

Mom served me hot soup and grilled cheese sandwich as she talked of a huge deal she'd made that day. She was in such a chattering mood, I decided to spring the idea on her.

"I want a dog," I said. "Someone to keep me company when you aren't here."

Mom stared at me. She almost dropped her sandwich as she carried it from the stove toward the table. "CJ, we talked about this when we left Dallas and you wanted to bring Twain. A dog would never be happy in an apartment."

"That was your logic," I said. "The truth is, I would take the dog out every morning and night when I walk. The river isn't so far away."

Mom squirmed in her chair. "Do you know how hard it is to rent a nice apartment if you have a pet?"

I smiled at her. I wanted to say, "Now we're getting to the gut of things, right Maggie? Me having a dog would make YOUR life a little more complicated. We wouldn't want that, now would we?" But I just kept staring at her.

"I've made an appointment tomorrow morning with a counselor in town." She handed me an appointment card.

"This tragedy at school has you in . . . shock. I don't know how to talk to you about it, so I'm getting you some help."

"Help, huh?" I said it with a sarcasm that Maggie couldn't miss. "You and Dad coming?"

I looked down at my grilled cheese sandwich and soup, willing them to disappear. Eating seemed suddenly like one more thing I 'should do'. I stood and gave my mother one last hard look, then went into my bedroom and slammed the door.

Sitting on the bed, curled up with my pillow, I remembered the counselor Mom and Dad sent me to in Wichita. They knew something was wrong, but it never occurred to them to sit and hold me, to tell me they were sorry my life had become insane, to cry with me and ask if they could help.

Instead, they sent me to this pompous ass of a school counselor. "Here, we screwed her up, now you fix her."

Of course it didn't work. I tried talking to him, but he brushed aside every single thing I tried to say about the divorce and how it messed me up. He gave me this line about taking responsibility for my actions.

I found out by accident that the counselor was going through a nasty divorce of his own. So I decided to be a smart ass.

"You aren't about to believe that the reason I'm screwed up is my broken home. Because if you believe that then you'll have to accept the fact that you're screwing your own kids up as we speak."

"Get out, you little bitch!" he screamed, jumping up from behind his desk.

He actually called me a bitch! I loved it. "The truth hurts doesn't it?" I asked, taking my time leaving. He followed me out into the hall calling out more bad names.

I told Mom about it, just to get even with her for sending me. Maggie was on the phone within the hour.

A week later I saw the counselor packing up the stuff in his office. I stuck my head in and smiled. "Taking responsibility for your actions?"

He threw a book at me. I laughed so hard I nearly wet my pants.

Scrunching down beneath my quilts, I covered my head with the pillow and tried to meditate. After awhile, I slipped into a restless sleep filled with snatches of dreams.

Bandit was beneath me and Twain was beside me and we were running along the river. I reached to give my pony a loving pat on the shoulder, but his dark brown coat and black mane had changed. He was golden and his mane was white. I looked down at Twain. His short red-brown coat was black and white. It wasn't Bandit and Twain. I was riding the golden palomino that Jacob loved and it was Prophet running beside us.

"Someday I'll ride free. Someday I'll ride free." I sat up with a jolt, still whispering the words. I got to my feet in a kind of daze. I thought about what I'd said to Mom earlier. 'I'd rather live alone.'

Standing in the darkness of the bedroom, something wild rattled through me like the clattering of autumn leaves across frozen ground. The snake of anger in my gut reared its head and worked its way around, up into my thoughts until my breath came in short gasps. The wind of change blew into my soul, like the velvet, sweet smell of spring rain.

I stepped forward and pushed the sliding door of my closet open. Burrowing my way to the back, behind all the suitcases and boxes and clothes, I felt slick leather and yanked my old saddle out of its hiding place

Sitting in the middle of the floor, I ran my hands lovingly over the rawhide horn, the worn leather seat, the dirt-crusted stirrups and sat with it in my lap for a long time. I reached back into the closet, pulled out the bridle, blanket and my sweat-stained felt hat.

My childhood possessions caused strong, confident memories to flash before me.

"I'll do it," I said, in a whisper, sitting in the dark. The words spread through me like cool medicine soothing the hot snake of anger. "I'll do it for us, Jacob. Ride free."

I tossed the saddle aside, stood and flicked on the bedroom light, and began grabbing things from the closet. I'd need my canteen, the canvas saddle bags, a flashlight, my rain slicker, my pistol. "I'll travel light, with just bare necessities. Ride fast."

Then, digging into the bottom of my dresser drawer, I pulled out the small cedar chest with the painting of the river on its cover. Jacob had made the box in his shop class and given it to me for Christmas. He painted the rough landscape with oils from his art class. "It's of my sacred place near the river. Where we met."

The box was my most treasured possession. Opening it, I looked at the hundred dollar bills, but couldn't force myself to touch them. It was the money I'd made on the sale of my pony. The eight crisp bills had stayed in the box for five years, untouched. I had made an oath to Bandit never to touch the 'blood money'.

The day Mom handed them to me, I cried. Tears gushed out of me so fast, I had no way of stopping the flood.

"I don't want it," I choked, and I wouldn't reach out my hand to take the money. Later she'd put the bills on the dresser at our first apartment in Houston. I'd left them in that same place and refused to touch them when we'd moved the second time to Amarillo, then to Wichita.

Mom took the money from apartment to apartment and put it back on my dresser. And so it had gone until Tulsa, until Jacob had given me the box last Christmas. The box was so special, it seemed rude not to have something valuable in it. But I didn't break my oath to Bandit. I didn't touch the bills. Instead, I'd used a hanger and slid the money off the dresser into the box.

I placed the box in one side of my saddle bags. I'd have to pay for the paint pony and have money for food.

I walked over and turned the light off, sat on my bed and looked out at the moon.

I swallowed the knot of pain in my throat when I thought of breaking the oath to Bandit. "I know you'll understand, old friend. If I don't pay for the pony, they'll be after me. But no one could ever take your place in my heart." Then I pushed my mind off of the past and toward the immediate future.

It had been a long time since I'd slept out beneath the stars. Oklahoma in May would be wet but warm. I envisioned myself along the Arkansas River, with the pony and Prophet, picking our way through the darkness. My animals would be my family and the river would be my home. The thought burned me with a passion for things past.

IV

The gentle sound of rain whispered against the roof of the apartment and I opened my eyes to the soft morning light. I snuggled deeper into the covers for a moment and let out a contented sigh. Jacob was reaching for me with that look of intensity in his green eyes. I blinked into wakefulness with my mind struggling between two worlds and weariness filtered over me.

Then Jacob's voice spoke the words in my memory, 'I will ride free'.

I sat bolt upright in bed, tossed covers aside and began to look for warm clothes.

I will get my things all together after Mom leaves. Go to town and buy some basics. Get a map and decide which direction to go. Then I'll catch the rancher and pay for the pony. Tell him I'll pick the paint up tomorrow. Tomorrow's Saturday, which means Mom will leave early, work a half day then come get me for a late breakfast. If I leave tonight after she goes to bed, I'll have around fourteen hours before she realizes I'm gone. I plotted to myself as I dressed in jeans and sweatshirt.

A tinge of guilt pinched me when I walked out into the kitchen and looked at Mom. *Poor Maggie. She has no clue how long I've been miserable. Her life is so focused on her job, I could build an atomic bomb in the middle of the living room floor and she'd step over it and say, "That's nice, dear."*

Do you know how hard it is to find a nice apartment if you have a pet? Yeah, Maggie, you do have your priorities. Now I won't stand in the way of them.

"Have some fresh blueberries on your cereal," Mom said, as the phone rang.

I dumped a generous amount of Cheerios into the bowl and covered them with blueberries. I wasn't hungry, but I had new motivation to eat.

"Hi, Penny." Mom's voice rang with enthusiasm from the living room as she greeted her best friend in Dallas. "Can you believe it? The asshole. We have a hearing in two weeks. I have no idea. Yeah. Yeah. Let the bastard go for it. It'll be a cold day in hell before CJ lives with them. I'll see to it."

Mom came back in, peppered her cereal with fresh, wild blueberries and smiled at me.

I stared at her and wanted to scream, "Do you think I'm deaf, Mom? Do you ever stop to think that the way you talk about Dad affects me? That asshole-bastard is my father, for God's sake." The burning snake in my gut lifted its head and began to hiss flames of anger.

I thought about Jacob. How many things had eaten at him day after miserable day? A father who didn't even care if he was alive. A mother who stood by and allowed a stranger to treat her own son like dirt.

"Your appointment is at 10:00. Don't forget," Mom said. "I have to run. I'm showing a $300,000 estate today and I think I have an interested buyer. If I make the deal, we can do Italian or try that new steak house everyone is talking about."

Then she was gone and I was rinsing the purple milk from my cereal bowl. When I looked out the kitchen window above the sink, I could see the rain had stopped. Water dripped from the roof of the apartment and far away a brilliant rainbow stretched in a perfect arc over the distant highway.

The rainbow beckoned to me. I thought of Jacob, how happy he would have been to leave with me. I pictured his green eyes narrowing and a shy grin lighting up his somber face.

I thought about the first time he'd touched me. It had been that day after I hid in the closet and he took me to his tee-pee. After he sang his song of sadness and my tears dried, he looked at me with his intense green eyes for a few lingering moments, then offered his hand. I took it and we sat, connected in our sorrow, for ever so long. It wasn't a demanding touch though, just a gentle offering of friendship, of understanding each other without words.

I pushed the memory back. I couldn't bear one more night in the apartment. The thought of a pompous counselor sitting behind a desk staring at me with a condescending smirk made me toss the cereal bowl in the sink and walk toward my bedroom.

"I won't wait until Saturday."

The phone was ringing and I stood over it, waiting for the answering machine to reveal the caller.

49

"Connie Jean, it's your dad. If you're there, pick up, please."

I reached for the phone, hesitated, then grasped it firmly in my hand. It was only right that I talk to Dad one last time.

"Hi, Dad."

"Are you OK, sweetie?"

"I'm fine."

"I'm sure your mother has told you by now. About the custody hearing."

"Yeah."

"I'm doing it for your own good, Connie Jean. I'm worried about you."

"It's too late to worry," I wanted to say. "It's been too late for quite awhile." But the words wouldn't come. Instead, I drew a picture on the note pad of me hanging from a tree with a rope.

"Connie Jean, it'll be OK. We'll get you back here, I'll find a place in the country. You can have another horse and a dog and . . . "

"Sure Dad."

"I'm just sorry you have to go through the whole court ordeal again."

"Yeah, well I'm used to it, you know." I crumpled the drawing in my hand and held it tight with my fist.

Hanging up the phone, I stood for the longest time and stared. "Have a great life, Dad. You and Cindy."

I walked into the bedroom and retrieved the cedar box. Holding it in my lap, I opened it and looked at the money for a long time. Biting my lower lip until it stung, I reached quickly, grabbed the bills and stuck them deep into my jacket pocket.

At the grocery store I bought tins of sardines, beef jerky, tuna, crackers, dried fruit and a block of cheese. I grabbed a cheap can opener, a small sauce pan, aluminum coffee pot and coffee. I dropped a spiral notebook and some ink pens onto my pile. *There will be lots of time to write.* The thought pleased me and I envisioned myself writing a novel, sitting on the river bank, serene, with only my dog and pony near by.

As I walked the aisles, my mind went over the things my grandfather and I used on our many camping trips up the river. The big difference, I wouldn't have a pack animal, so I had to keep my supplies to a minimum and find a way to restock from time to time. I'd gut the coffee pot and throw away its insides, boil water and throw in grounds for camp coffee. The pot could serve a dual purpose for boiling water to clean my dishes.

At the hardware store I bought a cheap aluminum fork, knife and spoon, a tin cup and plate, matches, a lighter, tarp, some fishing line, hooks and a good filleting knife. Standing outside on the street, I thought about everything I had and didn't have to have. Satisfied, I walked back to the apartment and began to pack.

The supplies that wouldn't fit into my saddle bags I stuffed into my back pack. I lifted my saddle, bags, bridle and all onto my left shoulder and grabbed my sleeping bag to see if I could handle the load. I retrieved my pistol, loaded the chamber with shells, then replaced it in the leather holster.

Smiling to myself, I put the things down and walked into the kitchen.

"Mom & Dad", I wrote on a sheet of yellow lined paper. A thousand thoughts began to rush into my mind and the anger in my gut burned. "My childhood ended with the divorce. That part of myself was lost forever. I'm declaring myself an adult now, ready to face all of my problems alone."

I started to add something about not worrying and that I didn't know for sure where I was going, but a big part of me just didn't give a damn if I ever saw either of them again.

Propping the note up between the crystal salt and pepper shakers, I made up my mind not to dwell on the parting. Mom would be home in approximately six hours. If I was lucky and could find the man and pay him for the pony, I'd be well on my way by then. If for some reason I couldn't, I'd stash my saddle and things in Jacob's tee-pee and wait until morning.

When I started through the brush, I couldn't quit thinking about Jacob. I tried to fight back the thoughts, but they battered their way forward. *You must have felt this exact same way, Jacob. Fed up with it all, hating your parents. That's why you talked so much about leaving, riding free. Why didn't you make me understand? I was so stupid.*

I stopped among the dripping trees and stood with all my gear. *We could have left together, Jacob.* The thought throbbed in my temples until I cried out an Indian squall. I screamed it, from the deepest part of my gut, like a wounded animal, then ran with my saddle and gear the rest of the way to the river.

When I stopped, my breath was coming in gasps.

Prophet met me bouncing in little circles. I dropped my saddle, packs and sleeping bag and wilted onto them with ragged breaths. "He didn't do it," I said, taking the dog in my arms. "Our Jacob couldn't have done such a thing."

Saying the words brought relief, so I kept talking. "It was the jocks. They somehow started bullying him and something bad happened. One of them had a gun and things got out of hand. Jacob got shot somehow."

Reaching for the table scraps in my pocket, I let Prophet eat as I revealed my plan. "We'll eat a lot of catfish from the river, broiled like you and Jacob used to."

When he finished eating, he put his front paws on my knee and looked up with this knowing expression on his face. I had the uncanny feeling that in that moment he was giving his trust and loyalty to me.

I took out the map and examined my options. Running my finger northwest, I followed the crooked blue line of the Arkansas river toward the towns of Pawnee, Pawhuska, Ponca City.

I thought of Jacob, how he would have loved to be with me. The towns were all named after Indian tribes.

The area between the towns was sparsely populated. It would be easy to stay hidden if I stuck close to the thick brush along the Arkansas River. Excitement began to build in me as I took a red pen and ran a line along the river going north.

"Fairfax." I said, "the old McGee homestead." I hadn't been back to Grammy and Pa Pa's place in a long time, but just the thought of it brought a smile. The 'homestead' held precious memories.

"Pa Pa used to take me camping along the creeks and rivers. We fished from the many ponds and ate watermelon near the creek on warm summer nights." I talked to Prophet and he listened intently.

"I know that country, Prophet. There are a thousand hiding places. Lots of channel catfish, blackberries and persimmons."

Saying the words caused a surge of emotion. My fingers shook as I made my red line curl around the Arkansas River and stop near Fairfax. I put an X on the spot northwest of town near the old homestead.

"I'm comin home, Pa Pa."

The loss of my grandparents still overwhelmed me. I didn't think of them often, because thoughts of them were too painful. Everything about them had been secure and loving.

One day I asked my grandmother how she met Pa Pa.

"At church," Grammy said as we sat snapping string beans. "Things were different then. Church was the only way to meet people and our dating all revolved around church socials. Dating used to be such fun. We were all carefree and happy. And, we had no pressure to have sex."

Staring at my grandmother, I almost dropped my handful of beans. Grammy was very religious and never spoke of such things. Later that night on the top bunk, with the wind fluffing the curtains, I thought about what she said and a part of me craved that simpler age. I imagined myself snuggled in between family and church like a little chick beneath a hen's feathers, and I quickly fell into a most peaceful sleep.

Grammy died just after I turned thirteen. Pa Pa didn't last six months after that. At my grandfather's funeral, Dad said, "Father couldn't face the reality of the world without Mother in it." The old place was abandoned now, the house falling in shambles.

My mind went back to the day Dad made the announcement about the divorce. "Your mom and I have decided to separate, we're filing for a divorce."

"But . . . we'll all be staying on the farm?" I asked.

Dad's head dipped and the muscles in his jaws clenched. "Your mom wants to move away from Dallas."

"But . . . " I stood in shock as a thousand questions swarmed around me like angry bees. "What about my friends, Dad? What about Bandit and Mark Twain?"

"It's going to be a rough change for all of us," Dad said, "but we'll get through it."

"I want to talk to my Pa Pa," I said, squinting my eyes toward Dad. "I need to talk to my grandfather about this." I said the words with all the authority my ten year old voice could command. "Pa Pa will know what to do."

Dad tried to ignore me, but in the end, when I wouldn't be silenced, he drove me the long hours from the outskirts of north Dallas to Fairfax.

"Pa Pa," I said, the minute I walked into the old farm house, "you have to talk to them."

My grandfather took me to the corral and without one word, we saddled two horses. We rode for an hour in silence. When he finally stopped and dismounted at the edge of the river, he knelt down and began to cry. Unashamed of his grief, Pa Pa took the red handkerchief he always carried in his back pocket and mopped at the tears on his face.

"Those two parents of yours, they won't listen to me."

"They can't get a divorce," I said. "Why would they do such a stupid thing?" Then, in my child's mind, I remembered something from the Bible Grammy had read to me. If it came from the Bible, who could argue with it? "When two people are joined together, only God can separate them."

Pa Pa began to walk along the creek and I followed. As usual, he thought quietly for a long while before he spoke. "Well, I reckon God meant it that way, honey. But it sure takes a lot of work for people to stay together. These days, people won't do the work, they want some easy way out."

"They can't do it, I won't let them."

My grandfather ignored my tantrum and continued. "Parents . . . aren't very smart sometimes," he said. "They lose sight of what's important. That's why God made grandparents. We're smarter. We know children are the most important thing on earth." He stuffed his handkerchief back in his pocket.

"But can't you tell them, Pa Pa? Can't you tell them I'm important?"

He took me up in his arms. "I could, CJ, but they wouldn't listen. Unfortunately young ears don't hear very well. Most of us have to learn the hard way, it takes time."

I worked a stick between my fingers as I dwelt for a moment on the memory. "Pa Pa's place is the closest thing to home I have left," I told Prophet.

Prophet agreed with an 'erf' and bounced down the path that led to the corral. I knew Jacob was right about the dog. He understood more than most people.

I untied my pack and saddle bags from the saddle, took off my backpack, slung my bridle over one shoulder and grabbed my saddle. My heart pounded in anticipation. It had been a long time since I'd held a pair of reins in my hand.

The paint nickered when he saw Prophet running up the dusty path. I felt my breath begin to come in short gasps as emotion choked me. Thoughts of Bandit came into my mind, but I fought to block them out. The bulge of bills in my front jacket pocket felt like lead over my heart as I stopped and stared through the corral.

"Hi fella." The moment the words left my lips the pony took a step forward, looking at me with his warm eyes. He took another step and stretched out his neck. I reached out to him, offering the tips of my fingers. *"Are you even trained?"* I thought and the question caused me to grin. The idea of taking off on a wild pony amused me. *"Well, if you aren't, we'll find out soon enough."*

I slid in between the boards of the corral and stood facing the golden paint. I ran my hands over him with caution. He wasn't skittish, but to my knowledge, Jacob hadn't ridden the paint. I had no idea if the pony had ever seen a saddle.

"You want to ride free?" I asked him, letting my hands slide over his withers down under his smooth belly then up his flank to his rump.

The bridle hung on my shoulder and the snaffle bit

clinked when I pulled it off and held it close to the pony's head. "Ever seen one of these?" I asked, putting my right arm slowly over his neck and slipping the bit toward his lips.

The pony took the bit eagerly, opening his jaws and slipping into the bridle as if it was an invitation he'd been waiting for. I let out a sigh. "Yeah, you've seen that before," I said, fastening the neck strap of the bridle and leading him a few steps toward the fence where I'd hung my saddle.

My confidence soared. If he'd been bridled and was that familiar with a bit, chances were he'd been ridden many times. I showed him the blanket. He smelled it with a whiff and acted undisturbed. I rubbed the blanket up against his withers and slid it slowly onto his back. When he didn't react, I knew I had it made. He stood quietly while I placed the saddle evenly on the pad and began to cinch the girth.

I could sense an eagerness in him and felt my own heart begin to beat with a hammering slam. I led him around the small corral once then tightened the cinch. "Well, let's see your stuff."

Holding the left rein short in my left hand, I put my left foot in the stirrup to test his reaction. He stood obediently, so I quickly mounted.

Sitting, holding the reins in my hand, I thought instantly of Pa Pa. I had overheard a conversation one morning between him and my Dad.

"Connie Jean is out of control, she's just plain wild, father." My dad's voice came from the kitchen and I stopped in the hallway to listen.

As usual, my grandfather didn't respond for a moment.

I heard him set his coffee cup down on the table. "Well, I seem to remember a time when someone else went through that age."

"It's different than what I did," my father barked. "She's running with a bunch of thugs, girls who've been in trouble and I'm afraid she'll get involved with drugs."

"Have you talked to her?"

"She won't listen to me."

His words burned me. I had tried talking to them many times, wanted to confide in them, but they were the ones who wouldn't listen. They were always too busy thinking of advice.

"Well," Pa Pa said, "she has a good heart and she's from good stock. She's just . . . reaching for the reins, that's all."

My mind floated slowly back and I smiled. I rubbed the leather between my fingers. My grandfather's faith in me had never waivered.

"I won't disappoint you, Pa Pa."

Settling myself comfortably in the saddle, I clicked my tongue to the gelding and he stepped forward. After two rounds, I kissed to him and he went into a fast trot that I encouraged into a slow canter. I said "Whoa," and he stopped so fast I fell forward in the saddle.

I patted him on the shoulder. "You graduated high school and went to college somewhere, didn't you?"

"One of the best around." The masculine voice caught me completely off guard. I was shocked to see an old man standing by the corral, watching me.

We stared at each other. My face flushed with embarrassment. I had no right to be riding someone's horse without asking. But I knew he was for sale. Jacob had pointed out the fading sign on the side of the splintery corral.

"Sorry I tried him out without asking," I said, walking the paint up to the fence.

"Well, if you was to take off on him, I reckon I'd have you hung for horse stealin." The man grinned wide at his joke and showed chewing tobacco between his rotting teeth.

I thought about my sketch on the note pad that morning and the idea of being an outlaw suddenly appealed to me. I smiled back. "How much?" I asked, knowing that time was important and I had to make good use of it.

"He's from a great line of quarter horses and racin paints. Got some Jet Deck blood in him and Rocket Bar. Sent him to a trainer over in Tulsa, Drew Brown. Heard a him? One a the best cuttin horse trainers around."

"No, sir. But I believe you. I can tell he's been to school."

"He can run, too. Match raced him a couple a times on the bush tracks. Out-ran everything by two lengths. I have his papers in the house."

"No, that's OK. How old is he?" I tried not to sound impatient.

"Goin on five."

I rubbed the pony's neck. A discouraging dread settled into my thoughts. With his papers, track record and training, he'd probably want well over what I could offer. I'd spent almost a hundred bucks on supplies. My future could get grim without any cash.

"How much?" I repeated.

"I've been askin a thousand dollars. And that's cheap. He'd make a fine animal for most anything. Parades, ropin, barrel racin or just a good ranch horse. And he's kid broke. Gentle as a lamb."

I grinned. I'd been around the sale barn enough to know the lingo. I'd heard my grandfather give it right back.

"Well, he seems sound enough. But he's a little small. I'm not sure he'd hold up to the kind of riding I'd be giving him." I said the words convincingly, but it was a lie. I preferred a horse under fifteen hands. "I sure as hell wouldn't put a kid on him. He's too quick."

The old man tucked his dirty thumbs behind his overalls straps and showed his tobacco teeth. The sport of haggling appealed to him, I could tell. He propped one brogan boot on the fence and spit.

"You been around some, I can see. Tell you what I'll do. Just for you, I'll knock it down to $900."

I stared at him, backed the pony up and took him around the pen in a figure eight pattern. I was buying time, trying to think of what to say next.

"He's a fine one ain't he?" The old man hesitated, scratched his chin and then he made a fatal mistake. "I've only been tryin to sell him for a week or so. Once I advertise him, he'll be gone in a heartbeat."

I knew he was lying. The pony had been in the corral and for sale for at least four months. The "For Sale" sign was faded. It was spring and horses of every kind and color were available. "I'll give you six hundred. It's all I have."

He grinned and spit again. "Why, I might as well meat him out. I could do better."

I dismounted and began to loosen the cinch.

"Tell you what I'll do. If you got the six hundred with you, I'll take it now and you can pay me another two hundred within the month and we'll call it good."

A spark of excitement ignited my pulse. I had him going my way. I undid the saddle, slid it off and threw it over the top rail of the fence. Unbridling the pony, I turned, with no emotion whatsoever, and left the corral, starting down the path.

"Don't go away mad," the old man whined. "I might consider $750."

I stopped and thought about my circumstance. I had enough food to last maybe two weeks if I stretched it. I could catch fish along the way, probably find blackberries and maybe even raid a garden or two. I had to have the pony.

I put my saddle slowly down on the grass and reluctantly pulled the bills out of my pocket, stuffing one of them back in before I turned.

"Most people will bargain in a heartbeat if you flash bills in their faces." Pa Pa's words came to me.

I turned, walked several steps toward the old man, counting the six hundred dollar bills and flashing them. "Four hundred, five hundred, six hundred," I said, looking up at him. "I told you. It's all I have."

The man licked his lips and I could see him spending the money in his mind.

"Can't do it," he said, shaking his head.

Pa Pa's voice returned to me. "Turn and walk away. You can always go back." I started down the path, knowing that at some point, I'd turn and give him the last, crisp bill, leaving myself without a penny. To my relief, I hadn't taken three steps when he hollered.

"You're robbin me! Hope you can sleep at night after you steal this horse."

I walked back and pushed the money into his hands. For a moment, I watched the crisp bills disappear into his yellow stained paw and thought of Bandit. But I quickly made myself look up at my new pony. I started back into the corral.

"Need a bill of sale," I said, slipping the bit back into the gelding's mouth.

The old man looked surprised. "Right now? You ridin him off this minute?"

"Yes sir. That's exactly what I'm going to do."

"Well, Missy, you don't mess around, do you?"

With the hand-written bill of sale and the pony's transfer paper in my back pocket, I waved to the old man then mounted and rode the pony toward the river.

Prophet danced and yipped around the pony's feet, then cut out in wide circles around us both, jumping with enthusiasm.

"Yeah, that's a good, boy. Let's see just how much energy you have before this day's through," I said, luxuriating in the familiar surge of power between my thighs, the feel of leather in my hand.

At the tee-pee, I tied the saddlebags and sleeping bag behind the saddle, pulled on my backpack and had just swung up into the saddle again when I heard the voices.

"I know he's been down in here somewhere. Used to

spend most of his time heading off in this direction." The faces came into view between the trees before I could bolt. I stared at Drake and a county sheriff.

Digging my heels into the gelding's flank, I leaned forward. My pony jumped into a run.

"Stop her! That dog! I've seen that dog with Jacob." Drake's voice echoed loudly through the trees and I heard footsteps crashing through the brush behind me. Then I heard a yelp from Prophet.

I pulled my pony up and turned in the saddle. Drake had dived toward Prophet and managed to grab one back leg. Prophet jumped and yipped in pain.

"Come, Prophet!" I screamed, knowing he had only a few possible seconds to escape because the sheriff was running to help. Prophet swung his agile body around and clipped Drake's hand with his teeth, grazing him just enough to make the little man recoil.

The chubby sheriff ran toward me, sweat beaded on his broad forehead. Prophet tore out in front of the paint and I leaned forward and gave the pony his rein just as the sheriff reached for my left stirrup.

"I'll catch you! Count on it!"

The crashing behind us and the voices faded in a hurry, but I didn't pull the gelding up until we were more than a half-mile down river. When I finally reined him in, all of us sat in the silence and struggled for breath. The gelding's sides heaved and his nostrils flared. Prophet plopped into the grass and panted, I slumped over and tried to quiet my hammering heart.

"Damn it," I swore, "I didn't want anyone to know." But

then, as the silent woods engulfed us, I began to relax. "Drake doesn't know me. And even if they try to follow us, they'll never catch us."

The smell of sweat from the gelding flooded me with happy memories of riding. I leaned and patted his shoulder. "Best smell in the world," I said. "We're gonna do fine together." But I didn't allow myself to think of my new pony in terms of 'forever'. The memory of saying goodbye to Bandit still hurt too much. I couldn't ever fall in love with another horse.

By late afternoon, I pulled the gelding up beneath a huge grove of cottonwoods. I could hear the hum of the freeway just off to the south and knew we had to cross the long bridge that would lead us to the safety of the west bank of the river.

Dismounting, I loosened the cinch, replaced the bridle with a halter, and tied the gelding to a low hanging branch. "Stay," I commanded Prophet. Both dog and horse seemed eager for the rest. Prophet went to the ground, head on paws and looked at me. The gelding shifted his back legs so that one foot was relaxed, partially off the ground. "I'll be right back."

I walked to the edge of the woods and looked at the busy freeway. Struggling up the lower branches of an oak tree, I made my way to the very top and stared at the monster bridge ahead.

"Damn," I said out loud. The four lanes buzzed with late afternoon traffic. The cars and trucks were bumper to bumper and the cement walkway on the side was barely wide enough for a bicycle. Riding a horse across wouldn't be an easy task. Even an exceptional horse who wouldn't spook at the roaring traffic might get skittish half way across when he realized the frothing river was beneath him.

I stood in the tree for a long while and looked, knowing my other option could be even more dangerous. Maybe if I waited until the early morning hours, traffic would slow to a crawl. But I had to consider the possibility that someone would spot me. I knew my parents would eventually be looking.

Climbing down the tree, I walked closer to the bridge, staying in the cover of the trees. When I was against the river's edge, I stopped breathing and stared.

The Arkansas River was bank to bank from the spring rains. At least two hundred yards of raging, muddy water crashed down with a roaring intensity, slamming limbs and debris with it. I swallowed and took a ragged breath.

"Well, old girl, this is where you find out what kind of pony you bought." I smiled to myself when I thought of Bandit, my half-Arabian half-Morgan swimmer. Nothing delighted Bandit more than a good swim and he was never afraid of water. Many times when we transported Bandit to Pa Pa's place in the summer, I'd ride my pony straight for the muddy waters of the Arkansas River and jump in.

It was Pa Pa who taught me how to swim my horse. "It's our secret," he told me with a wink, "Grandma and your daddy might . . . well, they might worry if they knew."

Walking toward camp, I began to think out loud. "I'll have to search for a better place to cross. And if the gelding hasn't been in water . . . " I stopped and worry took over. "The pony could panic, flounder in terror and if I lose my hold on his mane, I could be in big trouble."

Slipping the bridle over my gelding's halter, I mounted. Thinking about the river wasn't going to make swimming it any easier. I had to get across the river. If I camped there for the evening, I'd never sleep worrying about what was ahead. Once we crossed and got on the west side, according to the map, we shouldn't have to cross again.

The sun glared from the western sky. I shaded my eyes with my hand and walked the pony up and down the river, weighing the odds.

"OK, friend. I can't make this decision, so I'll let you make it for me. We're crossing this river one way or the other."

Coming to a bend in the wild river, I pulled Vision up and stared. Half way across was a small island. If the paint wasn't a good swimmer or if he spooked, I'd have a safety net. I walked upstream from the island, knowing the raging water would sweep us down. I pointed the gelding toward the river. He took two nervous steps that let his front hooves sink into the sloshing river. I patted him on the neck.

"What do you think, little man? It won't be any easy job with the saddle on, but I have confidence in you." Prophet waded in. The current carried his light body out and slammed him several yards down stream. He swam frantically back, clawed his way up the bank, then looked at me and whined a warning.

"I know. It's scary. But it's one of two bad choices." I put my heels against the pony's sides and tried to coax him into the raging water. He snorted, pivoted and suddenly we were facing the opposite direction. I patiently turned him back and gently kissed to him, squeezing his sides with my legs. Again he turned and this time he danced nervously and snorted his objection, tossing his head.

"OK, I'll have to trust your judgement on this. But when you see the other option, you might change your mind."

I rode to the edge of the woods facing the monster bridge and dismounted. Unfastening the cinch, I pulled the saddle off and laid it in the deep grass. Taking the bridle off, I held the halter rope so the gelding could graze. He pushed his nose into the lush grass and pulled at it hungrily. For months he'd been held prisoner inside the small corral. I could tell by his eyes and the toss of his head, he liked the green grass and the freedom.

"That's right, you relax for awhile. We'll watch this old highway and see if she settles down a bit." I took out a piece of jerky and began to nibble at it, thinking I would wait to make camp until we crossed the bridge. I had little faith in the honesty of the old man, but prayed the gelding had been around traffic and noise.

"Match raced him a couple of times on the bush tracks." The old man's words came back to me with an image of the tobacco teeth.

"Well, fellow, if you've been around the race track, with loud speakers crackling and flags flapping, a few cars shouldn't bother you," I was trying to convince myself. The traffic didn't worry me as much as the water below. Sometimes horses reacted wildly to things over and under them.

"I have to quit calling you, fella. What's your name, any-way?" I reached for the papers in my back pocket. I read starting at the bottom with his markings, then let my finger go up, looking at the breeding of sire and dam, original owner. When my finger came to the top of the paper, I stared in disbelief at the words written under 'name'.

VISION OF LOVE

Goose bumps peppered my arms and I rubbed at them, hugging myself as I knelt in the grass. Prophet came to me, as if he knew what I'd just discovered. He pushed against my legs and his wet body felt cool against the afternoon warmth of the sun.

"I will call my dog Prophet. He was sent as a gift from the spirits to lead the people to see with the eyes in their heart. I saw it in a vision." Jacobs words echoed in my mind.

I stared back at the name, thinking I'd imagined it, thinking it should be a normal registered name, something basic, like Jets Easy Bar or Rocket Boy Go.

"Vision Of Love." I stood and walked to the pony. I let my hands travel across his body, the way I'd seen Jacob do a hundred times. "We're going to make it over that bridge and back to Osage County, to Pa Pa's and we're . . . "

I had no idea what else I intended to say, but in that instant, I had the distinct feeling I was doing more than running away. I was running toward something.

V

By seven o'clock daylight faded into a creamy puddle of orange in the western sky. The steady traffic on the interstate dwindled. I stood, considering the situation. Waiting until dark would be safer as far as being spotted, but if the gelding spooked in the middle of the bridge, headlights in the blackness might cause him to panic.

Slipping the bridle on, I tightened the cinch, checked all of my gear and mounted. "Vision," I said, patting his neck. "Remember, you had an option. This was your choice."

When we rode out into the open country that led to the highway, I had an urge to turn my pony and run back to the security of the trees. We were so vulnerable, so visible.

I guided Vision onto the narrow, cement walkway of the bridge and felt him tighten and hesitate beneath me. I patted him and urged him on, squeezing my heels against his flanks. Prophet walked in front of us and followed each car that passed with his eyes.

I began to whistle a song. "If you stay calm, your pony can sense it," Pa Pa always said. Vision relaxed beneath me and Prophet walked on as if he knew he were leading the way.

Halfway across the sound of the river began to roar beneath us. Vision snorted and tossed his head, but I didn't give in to his nervousness. Instead I began to sing as I rubbed his neck and encouraged him.

"You're doing swell."

Oncoming cars in the far left lanes didn't seem to bother Vision as much as the closer traffic going with us, zipping up from behind. Cars began to slow as they passed and people turned to stare. Worry surfaced in my thoughts. *Would they begin looking for me this soon? If Mom came home early, had she already called Dad? Would they call the police?*

Fifty yards before reaching the safety at the end of the bridge, a semi-truck with a piggy-back load of fuel came roaring past and blew his horn just as he was even with us. The bellowing rage made me put my feet deep in the stirrups and get a grip on the saddle horn. Vision bunched up. His knees trembled and he began to scramble beneath me. The hollow echo of his hooves sounded out over the river. I gathered the reins tightly.

"Whoa, whoa, boy, it's OK." The combination of the river, the bridge beneath his feet and the horn was too much. He leaped to the left onto the highway. Horns beeped and cars swerved as I tried to control him, but he started slipping. I pulled my boots from the stirrups just as he went down and was lucky the impact sent me forward on my feet.

I grabbed the reins and jerked Vision back up on the walkway. He leaped toward me, almost stepping on my right leg. I held him by the bit and began to talk. "Settle down now. It's OK. Settle down." My mouth was dry and my heart pounded in my ears as I began to walk.

Prophet remained calm through the entire ordeal. He stood in front on the walkway. Vision jumped and scrambled for several more yards, but I clung to him as I watched the huge truck disappear over the distant hill.

"Moron," I said, through clenched teeth.

"Always has to be one." Pa Pa's words again came into my mind. "A smart ass that will come along and have to be cute. If you aren't ready, CJ, it could get you killed."

When we reached the other side, I mounted Vision and headed straight toward the safety of the trees. As the blackjacks and scrub oak began to embrace us, my gelding's nervous prance settled into a walk.

"We made it, buddy," I said, rubbing his neck. "We made it."

The woods were still damp from the morning rain, so it took awhile for me to get a campfire going. I hobbled Vision and watched him struggle for a few minutes against the restraint, then settle into grazing.

"If you weren't a strong pony with a good mind . . . " I let the words and the worry slowly leave my mind.

When water began to boil in the pot, I tossed a handful of coffee into the bubbles. I opened a tin of sardines, sliced some cheese and placed crackers on my plate. I ate slowly, savoring every nibble. Bullfrogs from the river croaked in the coolness of the early evening and fireflies winked.

73

I finished half of the food then slid the plate toward Prophet who waited nearby. I sipped coffee and watched as he took one bite of sardine at a time, then the cheese and ate the crackers last. He'd always been a polite eater. Jacob used to eat his fill of catfish, and then hand Prophet his share. No matter how hungry Prophet was or how long he had to wait, he didn't grab his food or suck it down.

"You're a gentleman." I rubbed him behind the ears and he kept eating, but his tail flicked in response to the compliment.

I sat for a long time, looking into my small fire, sipping the coffee. A peaceful feeling of independence filtered over me. "I'm riding free, Jacob," I said. My voice thickened and the heavy iron coldness gripped my shoulders and made me shiver.

I reached quickly for my notebook and pen. Maybe if I wrote everything, everything I could remember about him and about us, maybe then I could somehow begin to make sense of it all.

My mind drifted back to the days after Jacob had first held me. The memory was bittersweet. My feelings for him began to change that day, standing in the closet, listening to Drake abuse him. I'm not sure exactly what I felt, empathy maybe, but more than that.

I started to write.

My visits to the river to see Jacob turned into the most important events of my days. He was all I thought about at school, and at night, curled beneath the security of my warm quilts, I could feel the intensity in his green eyes, see the way his sandy hair ruffled in the wind like wheat just before harvest. I could barely wait each afternoon to rush in from school, change clothes and meet him at the river.

But even I didn't know it was love. Then came that golden afternoon in late October when I realized my feelings went beyond friendship.

I had had a really lousy day at school and came home, wanting to run straight to the river. Mom insisted we go to the mall for shopping. She got really irritated with me because I didn't want to 'hang out' with her and she left angry.

When I walked to the river, Jacob stood, shirtless, with an old hawk feather hanging from his shoulder length hair. He had been in the river and the sun filtered through the red-gold trees making the water glisten like diamonds on his tan body.

I'd never seen Jacob without a shirt. I was shocked to see that beneath his thin leanness, were tight, strong muscles.

I watched as he went into some kind of martial art routine, kicking his legs up as high as his head, then turning, his hands flicking in front of him, like windmill blades. He spun around, dived, and jumped with an incredible display of speed and agility. The sight left me breathless and slightly dizzy. When he was finished, and bowed to his invisible audience, I felt my legs weaken beneath me and I slumped onto the ground.

For a long time I sat, amazed at the secret I'd just discovered. Jacob Johnson was not helpless, weak and afraid. He had a deep inner strength that took him beyond wanting to physically fight. Every day he suffered the torment of the athletes at Fremont High, knowing he could stop them. The secret made my cheeks burn and something very subtle tugged at my heart.

When I finally did get the nerve to approach Jacob, I struggled with the right words. "I . . . saw you, just now. That was awesome. Where did you learn it?"

He smiled at me. It was that slow easy grin that sometimes sneaked like a drifting shadow across his face. Part of me wanted to slide into his arms, embrace him, and never let go, but the memory of Wichita made me step back.

"My Uncle John came once for a visit. He showed me things, gave me a book. I practice every day."

I unrolled my sleeping bag and sat. When Prophet crowded up next to me, I hugged him.

"If only I'd told him," I said. Prophet whined and scooted closer and I squeezed him. When the ache in my heart became unbearable, I forced myself to think of something else.

I thought of my parents, arguing at the apartment. Dad had probably flown up by now and the two of them were screaming at each other, trying to place blame. I had no regrets about leaving. The only regret I had was that I hadn't left sooner, hadn't suggested the idea to Jacob.

"Mom and Dad will probably call the cops," I told Prophet, "but it doesn't matter. If we stick near the river, they'll never find us. After a few weeks maybe they'll get tired of looking and get interested in something else."

"Mom will probably be on the computer immediately,

making some kind of poster with my face on it. HAVE YOU SEEN THIS CHILD?"

"That's how they still look at me. Like a child," I said to the night. "Dad will try to outdo Mom, probably hire a private detective." I turned to Prophet and he listened. But I knew that since I'd left a note saying I was leaving, the cops would just call me a runaway and lose interest after awhile.

"They've done what they wanted in their lives now it's time for me to do the same." Prophet looked up at me attentively but didn't move his head from my knees.

"The thing that bothers me most about the divorce is that they aren't either one better off. Happier. They weren't so bad together. Dad just wanted Mom home more and it really upset him that she was driven toward a career. But Mom didn't do much to soothe his ego. Mom wasn't big on shoring people up. Still, they had lots of good things, lots of years invested. If they'd worked at it . . . things would be real different right now."

I began to take deep, even breaths, the way Jacob had taught me. "Breathe in through your nose, slowly, deeply, exhale, let all thoughts evaporate from your mind." I could hear his words whisper into my ear. The sound of his voice and my breathing put me back in a sweet space and I slipped into my sleeping bag, cuddled my dog and yawned.

The next morning, Vision grazed near me. When I opened my eyes, he put his white nose down close to my hair and whiffed out a soft breath.

"Morning," I said. He jumped back and stood, straddle

legged, with a surprised look in his dark eyes that made me laugh.

Prophet, caught in the fun, circled around Vision and me in teasing circles, barking, then bounded into my arms as I unzipped the sleeping bag.

The sun shone bright in the eastern sky as I made a small fire and warmed the coffee from the night before. Sipping from the tin cup, I held it close and luxuriated in the warmth. I knew I'd be shedding my jacket by early afternoon.

I dug into my saddlebags for the rubber curry comb I'd decided to bring. Haltering Vision, I brushed him with long, deep strokes, sending the loose winter hair floating on the cool wind. I curried his long, white mane until it shone translucent in the light.

"You're a beautiful man," I told him, "with a big heart. You did swell on the bridge last night. The worst part is behind us."

I left Vision tied and commanded Prophet to stay while I walked several hundred yards to the clearing that looked down on the highway, back toward the bridge. Pausing by a huge cottonwood, I munched the handful of dried fruit I'd chosen for breakfast.

This is going to be the life, I thought. *Making my own decisions. Living with my dog and pony. Writing every day.* For a moment I thought of what I'd left behind. I wouldn't have to return to Fremont where a hundred haunting memories would face me every day. I would no longer be caught in the middle of my parents' war.

But as I walked aimlessly toward the top of the hill, I

knew, deep in my gut, I hadn't gotten away free. Would never be able to leave the tragedy behind.

I reached the crest of the hill and fell to the ground, my face against the dirt. The dried apples in my hand fell into the grass as I clawed my way up, inch by inch, staring down at the scene below me in disbelief.

On my end of the bridge, a roadblock flashed. A trooper was stopping cars going west while a traffic cop directed the east bound vehicles out and around the road-block. I let my eyes devour the swarm of cops canvassing the entire area on foot. Highway patrolmen, sheriffs, city cops dotted the ditches on both sides of the river.

"My God," I choked, slithering down the hill, "are they looking for me?" I crawled back to the safety of the trees and with shaking fingers, quickly saddled Vision. I covered my fire slowly with dirt, to create less smoke.

"We have to ride," I told them. Mounting, I kicked Vision into a slow gallop along the river's edge. It wasn't until noon, when my stomach growled with hunger, that I pulled him to a halt and dismounted in the safety of the thick brush.

"Probably an escaped convict or something," I told Prophet as we sat near the river and munched cheese and crackers. But an image of the sheriff's broad face loomed in front of me. "I'll catch you! Count on it!"

My mind wouldn't rest. *If my parents reported me missing last night wouldn't the cops wait twenty-four hours before they even began to look? I'm sure I've heard that somewhere. They wouldn't set up a road block or send out half the Tulsa police force for me Would they?*

The uneasy feeling wouldn't leave me though, and by early dusk I searched for a camp site deep in the thick woods. After I unsaddled, brushed and hobbled Vision, I pulled the map from my saddle bag.

We had to be near the northeastern edge of Keystone Lake. According to the map, if we hung near the river, we could avoid the small towns ahead. Following the river added extra miles. Its meandering would slow my journey, but I couldn't leave the security of the trees. "And besides," I said, ripping off a piece of jerky and offering it to Prophet, "we aren't in a hurry."

After gathering limbs and breaking them into small twelve-inch sticks for a fire, I dug into my supplies for fishing line and hook. When I had my gear ready, I began to turn over rocks until I found a fat worm.

"In the summer when worms get too deep in the ground, grasshoppers and frogs are good catfish bait," I told Prophet.

I threw the line into the swirling, muddy water near the roots of an ancient willow tree. "Always look for a calm place, Pa Pa taught me. That quiet deepness is where the big boys like to live."

Sitting in the short grass on the river bank, I listened to Vision munching behind me. Sweet spring grass was abundant. Soon, when the relentless Oklahoma heat began to bear down, brutal in its intensity, there would scarcely be enough for the deer and wildlife to scrounge a meal.

Prophet hunted in the nearby brush for rabbits and field mice, pushing his nose into tight places, sniffing and sneezing. Every few minutes, he'd return to me, panting, glancing directly at my eyes, as if he were checking on my state of mind.

"That's a good boy," I told him on each visit. "Find you some supper in case I don't catch a fish."

I leaned against the trunk of the willow and watched Vision, thinking of days gone by. The clanking of his hobbles brought Kelly and Suze, my childhood buddies, to mind. Kell with her dashing Arabian stud and Suze with her mule. What a pair.

I wondered if the two of them were still riding the rolling hills northeast of Dallas. *Probably. But now instead of talking rodeo, they're talking about college and guys and life.*

"Wish you were with me," I said, thinking of all the many riding escapades the three of us had taken. All the hours we'd spent setting up barrels and poles in our arena, measuring, discussing it by the book. The hysterical early attempts we made at roping the calves in Dad's pasture. Then later, our ribbons and trophies from the local rodeos.

The good feelings all began to fade and I felt the old snake of anger twist in the pit of my stomach. *That life is gone. I'm not that carefree child anymore. Too much has happened. I won't ever be that innocent or pure again.*

I stood and tied my line securely to a low-hanging willow limb. "We better see exactly where we are." Prophet barked his approval.

Climbing inch by inch up the slender cottonwood, I tested each branch before putting my full weight on it. I was thankful for all the trees Jacob had made me climb, all the obstacle courses I'd followed him through the past six months. "If not for that conditioning," I said out loud to a blue jay fussing around my head, "I wouldn't make it five miles."

I thought about the extra pounds I'd put on before I met Jacob. How eating, sitting, watching TV had become my life after school. How depressed I'd gotten since Wichita.

Jacob became my personal trainer.

"I'm so fat," I told him one day when guilt settled over me because I'd gained ten pounds. "So fat, and I don't care now. I just eat more."

"I care," he said. "Come on, exercise will help your mind." Then he put me on the daily work out schedule that included running, tree climbing, swimming, and eating more protein and fewer carbs. By the end of the first week, I was aching all over, whining and being very vocal about the entire ordeal.

"This is crazy. I'm gonna die," I told him, falling into a heap on the ground after a run. " No wonder you are such a rail."

He gave me his rare smile and looked at me for a long time before he spoke. "You are gonna love you," he said.

The memory made me smile. "Oh, Jacob," I said, and the whispered words burned my heart, so I climbed faster.

From the uppermost branches of the tree I caught a glimpse of shimmering water. The setting sun cast a red-orange glare across the lake that made me squint. To the north, less than a half mile away, stood the lake front store. A Bud-Light sign competed with the sun to glare in the early dusk.

The sight of the small building brought back the memory of the drives Dad and I used to take from the apartment in Tulsa to my grandparents' farm. We'd leave the buzz of the city and drive nearly an hour without much conversation. It was after the divorce and just before Grammy died. There wasn't much good to talk about.

But after we turned off the turnpike and onto the two lane road that led north, Dad always pulled up in front of the small store.

"Want a little something, sweetheart? Last stop until we get to Grandpa's," he'd say.

I'd ask for a cup of the fresh cider the old man always sold. The sweet flavor had just a hint of cinnamon that stayed on my tongue all the miles toward Fairfax.

With a bitter sigh, I thought of the bad times that followed that sweet memory. Grammy's death, Pa Pa getting sick, my futile attempts to talk my parents into keeping the old home place.

"We can't just let some stranger buy it. Pa Pa worked his whole life to build that place."

"Honey, you aren't being realistic. You have school and then college. I hate to let it go as much as you, but I can't leave Dallas. We all have our lives to live."

"I'll wait until dark, leave Prophet with Vision," I said, starting down the tree. "Pick up a few supplies and some fresh water." But a newspaper was the most urgent thing on my list. I knew the last of the funerals would probably be that day, there would be more about the shooting, things I had to know. By now they must know that Jacob didn't do it.

My willow limb was dancing wildly when I approached the river. The line pulled hard to the left then circled and tugged to the right. Grabbing it, I knew immediately by the weight I had plenty of supper for Prophet and me. My heart raced as I wrestled the flopping fish against the bank and finally held him securely by hooking my index finger in his gills.

"Supper," I told Prophet, as he jumped around my feet and barked. I laughed. "You can't have him yet. We have to cook him."

An hour later, I gave most of my share of the fish to Prophet. I couldn't quit thinking about the funerals. How all of them but Jacob would have crowds of people to honor their deaths.

I should have waited. Gone to Jacob's funeral before I left. The words kept walkingg through my mind.

I took Prophet in my arms. "You stay," I told him. "You stay here with Vision. Understand? I'll be back as soon as I can."

When I walked to the edge of the camp site, Prophet whined, but didn't move from his place near my saddle. "Good dog," I assured him, walking on.

I waited across the highway in the trees for the last car to pull away from the store, then approached with caution. I hadn't seen the old couple who ran the store in over three years, I prayed they wouldn't recognize me. I bent and dusted my hands with dirt, rubbed it on my face and pulled my hat down.

Ducking through the door, I dived down the first aisle. Grabbing two cans of ranch style beans and a box of crackers, I walked to the end of dusty shelves and took a gallon of drinking water. I pulled my hat lower over my face when I approached the counter. Putting my items down, I reached for the daily paper and froze when I saw the huge letters across the front page.

GIRL SOUGHT IN CONNECTION WITH SCHOOL SLAYING

In the lower left hand corner was a vivid image of me, smiling my biggest smile. I ducked my head even more, pushed the paper in with my items and handed over the hundred dollar bill.

"Howdy," the old man drawled. "Well, it's a good thing you're givin me that big bill late in the day, otherwise I'd never be able to make change."

I couldn't talk, afraid my voice would come out in a squeak. My cheeks burned as he counted the money into my hand. It took what seemed like an hour for him to put the few items in a paper bag. He studied my face as he picked up the cans of beans one at a time and shuffled things around.

"Haven't I seen you somewhere before?" he finally said. The words made my heart slam as I reached for the brown paper bag.

Shaking my head and taking the groceries in my arms, I tried to walk nonchalantly out the door. My legs weakened beneath me as I went across the lot. I knew he was watching me. I stopped and turned.

The old man stood just behind the screen door, staring.

VI

Panic pumped through me. If he recognized me from the picture, if all those cops at the bridge had been looking for me, every move I made now was crucial. I couldn't allow the man to know where I was camped.

Instead of walking across the gravel road and heading straight to the open field south, I walked east, back toward Tulsa. I walked at an even, brisk pace, although my knees were weak. I continued without turning around until I was well out of sight of the store.

When I looked back and could barely see the faded red roof of the building, I cut quickly into the brush along the road and headed for the trees along the river. The moment the cool shade of the giant cottonwoods embraced me, I started running. My cans banged and water sloshed inside the sack. I doubled back toward camp, sprinting the entire way.

Vision nickered a welcome and Prophet dived into my arms when I crashed onto my sleeping bag. Gasping for breath, I jerked the paper from the sack and began to read in the light of the campfire.

IF YOU'VE SEEN THIS GIRL, PLEASE CONTACT THE TULSA COUNTY SHERIFF OR THE LOCAL AUTHORITIES AT ONCE. Fifteen year old Connie Jean McGee is now a suspect in the Fremont School Massacre.

Prophet squeezed up into my lap and crawled beneath the paper. I continued to read.

"Connie Jean, known as CJ to her friends and family, has now been linked to the shooter by Jacob Johnson's stepfather, Drake. Drake claims he knew of a secret hideout along the Arkansas River where his stepson hid a stray dog. A place where Jacob often went to practice strange, occult ceremonies that included painting his face and burning catfish over open fires."

I snorted in disbelief. "BURNING catfish. Give me a break. He ate fish because there wasn't anything in your house to eat. Stepfather? Stepson? They weren't married."

I squinted closer to the paper. "Mr. Drake is a liar," I said, then struggled for a moment with the name. Jacob always called him Drake. I assumed all along, that was his first name. "Drake, Drake," I said.

"Drake claims he saw the girl running from the vicinity of the hideout on Friday, with his stepson's dog, that he describes as a black and white Border Collie. On Saturday, after spotting a flyer with Connie Jean's picture, Drake reported the connection to the sheriff."

As I read, the snake of anger twisted and burned. Mom had made a missing flyer with my picture the very night I left. Good old Mom, always efficient. She hadn't accepted my note at all. Now, thanks to her, I had an army chasing me.

"Connie Jean was mounted on a palomino paint horse

she apparently purchased from a Mr. Shank who lived nearby on the river.

"Mr. Shank says, and I quote, 'Yes, sir, she was in a hell-bent hurry, that gal was. Paid me in cash for the horse. Fifteen crisp one hundred dollar bills. Wondered where a kid that age came up with that kind of cash. Probably stole it, I'll betcha. Course, I didn't know that at the time. She wanted a Bill of Sale right on the spot, then she left, like she had a fire under her feet.'"

I couldn't keep from smiling, "You lying sack of shit," I said. "Fifteen hundred dollars?" I could picture the old man, grinning with the tobacco in his teeth, propping his foot up on the fence and adding the lies to make himself feel more important.

The article continued, "If you see this girl, call the police immediately. Eleven young people are dead and four others still on the critical list in the hospital after last week's school shooting rampage at Fremont High. Jacob Johnson's autopsy revealed that his system was free of alcohol and drugs."

"Jacob never did drugs or drank," I told Prophet. "He hated his mother's drinking so much. Remember how he'd bring bottles of her booze down to the river and break them against that old stump?" Prophet barked a reply.

"Alan and Maggie McGee have vehemently denied their daughter's involvement with the shooter, Jacob Johnson. They can offer no explanation for her running away, but claim she is not connected to the Fremont Massacre. The McGees have offered a $10,000 reward for their daughter's safe return.

I dropped the paper and let out a bitter sigh, "Thanks a lot Mom and Dad."

I stood and walked to the river's edge. *They can't offer an explanation for her running away.*

"No," I said, "because they are clueless about my life." The knowledge that they were probably reeling in shock gave me a tug of satisfaction.

"Not only did I know Jacob," I said to the roaring river, "I loved him and he is no more guilty than I am."

I knelt for a minute and worked a willow branch between my fingers as a flood of worry washed over me. Riding to my grandparents' place and hiding out, living a life of peace and quiet was going to be more complicated now. They'd probably never quit looking until they found me.

I recalled the look of determination on the sheriff's face when he almost grabbed me near Jacob's tee-pee. If he could catch me now, he'd be a national hero.

"I'm a fugitive," I told Prophet, who crawled back into my arms and nuzzled my neck. I let out a deep sigh and thought about my options.

Maybe I should just go back before they catch me. Turn myself in and tell them the truth. Drake is the one who should be a fugitive. Tell them about the abuse, the way the kids at Fremont treated Jacob.

But the idea of giving in to my parents' war, to the sheriff who thought he could catch me, being dragged into a situation where everyone demanded answers from me, fired me with resistance.

"No," I said, and thought of the first custody hearing between my parents.

"Connie, do you have a preference as to which parent you'd like to live with?" The judge asked the question so matter-of- factly, as if he were asking me to choose between peppermint or chocolate.

"No," I said, in the plush privacy of the judge's quarters, then walked into the courtroom and stared first at Mom then Dad. Both of them were looking at me with searching eyes, wondering. I sat in the courtroom and almost laughed.

I appreciated the irony. For the first time since the big divorce announcement, I had a voice. The opportunity to be heard. I'd yearned for a choice in the beginning, begged to be heard. But neither of them would listen to me for five minutes. Now it didn't matter.

"No," I said, jumping up and sending Prophet out of my lap. "I won't give in to their insanity. They'll never catch me if I stay near the river. Let them try."

I knelt by the river's edge and scooped mud onto my index finger. Streaking it in a jagged line across my fore-head and on my cheeks, I stood and began to scuff one foot in front of the other, singing out a guttural squall of rage and fear.

"Hai, hai, hi yi."

"I'll run for you, Jacob. Ride free. They'll never catch me." I sat, cross-legged and gave out the call of the mourning dove. "Awoo-woo-woo-woo. Awoo-woo-woo-woo."

When a crisp, lonely answer came, I looked out across the river, disbelieving. "Are you with me, Jacob?" I whispered. "What happened that day, Jacob? You have to tell me." I put my hands together and repeated the call.

91

"Awoo-woo-woo-woo. Awoo-woo-woo-woo."

But this time I sat in the darkness for a long time, waiting. The silence left me numb with grief.

Prophet let out a bark, circled me, then made a wide sweep in front of Vision, looked back and barked again. He was ready to run.

Three hours later, allowing Vision to pick his way through the underbrush close to the river bank, I settled into a half-daze, relaxed in the saddle, with the reins loose.

My mind replayed the day of the shooting over and over until I squeezed my head between my hands, trying to force the memories out. Finally, reining Vision to a stop, I pulled my notebook from my backpack and searched for a pen.

In Mrs. Mac's class, doing the assignments she'd given, learning to write from 'the inside out,' I had found a solace for my soul.

For six months, I'd kept a daily journal, pouring out my secret attraction to Jacob, the desires he stirred in me, the passion I'd never let him see. I revealed my anger toward my parents, my grief over losing Grammy and Pa Pa, the nightmare of Wichita. Writing always helped calm the demons in my mind.

I began to scribble in the moonlight as I rode. The letters were wobbly and the lines crooked and the strange look of them in the half-light gave me pleasure. "The Maze," I said.

'My dearest Jacob, I'm on Vision and Prophet is with me. We are riding free. I think often of your voice, the sadness in your song, how you longed to go back to The People. You were a warrior who had lost his pony, his people and his pride. Now, more than ever, I know how you felt.'

"Whoa, boy." I looked out over the muddy river that Jacob had loved so dearly. "Jacob," I said. "Jacob, I loved you. I loved you. Why didn't I tell you?"

The question left me aching with regret. I stared down into the frothing water and yearned to dive in. Let the muddy darkness embrace the pain, swallow me up and carry me to some mysterious place of peace with Jacob.

Prophet's barking snapped me out of the trance and I squeezed my legs gently against Vision's sides. He began to walk but stopped after only a few steps. I focused in the darkness and swallowed. A new, five-strand barbed wire fence stretched out in front of us, running down the steep bank into the water.

I turned in the saddle and my eyes followed the fence away from the river and in the dim light, I could see fence posts dotting up over the hill toward the highway.

I knew, staring back toward the water, I'd made my first big mistake. "I didn't bring wire cutters." I said out loud. I studied the situation and decided it was a bad place to introduce Vision to the river. The bank dropped off suddenly and the water looked deep.

Reining Vision around we walked to the edge of the woods. In the moonlight, I could see a brick home about a hundred yards away. In order to get around the fence, I'd have to ride up in front of the house and circle back to the safety of the river. From the highway in front of the house,

I could hear the buzz of an occasional truck and see headlights through the darkness.

Just as I nudged Vision out into the clearing, I became aware of a noise in the distance and first thought it to be a truck on the highway. Quickly the faint hum turned to a roar as a helicopter blasted down over the river, with a great sweep of light. I turned Vision back into the trees and dug my heels into his flanks. He leaped out in a dead run.

Vision fidgeted and his sides heaved as I reined him into a thicket of cedars. Prophet sat beside us, panting. The helicopter made a sweep above. It was so close the wind from the propeller blew Vision's mane. The gelding danced nervously as I held him and rubbed his neck. I slumped onto the saddle, making a smaller target for the flood light.

Within seconds the helicopter disappeared. I sat, cemented into the hiding place for thirty minutes, waiting. My heart hammered against my jean jacket pocket and my mouth turned to sand.

I reached for my canteen and drank slowly, then draped it back over the saddle horn. I walked my pony back to the edge of the woods and stared, once again, at the clearing ahead.

"Just do it," I said, hoping the helicopter had traveled far down the river and wouldn't return. I kicked Vision into an easy gallop and he obeyed. Still stressed from the copter, he fought the bit and lunged forward. I held him gently and forced myself to relax in the saddle. Finally he settled into a canter and we quickly covered the distance to the house.

Two big dogs barked, from the yard. Prophet met the

challenge, running the length of the fence, barking back.

"Prophet, come," I said, trying to command him in a firm, but low voice. Lights flicked on inside the house. "Come!" I screamed, giving Vision his rein.

We tore through the brush with no caution of limbs or stumps, jumping on the run, dodging. I headed Vision straight toward the safety of the river. We rode on and on through the dense thicket of sumac and blackjack. The deeper we worked into the maze, the safer I felt.

I didn't relax and rein Vision in until the sound of the river returned to my ears. After a brief rest, I nudged him forward. We rode on and on through the night. My legs began to ache and I pulled them out of the stirrups, stretching and then letting them dangle, but rode on.

I didn't allow myself to think of camp or rest until the first streak of daylight spread across the eastern horizon.

As I dismounted, the full impact of my situation and how it had changed hit me. I would not have the luxury of going anywhere near grocery stores where people might see me. I couldn't buy drinking water, so would have to boil water from the river. The open fields of good grass that bordered the river would now be an invitation for trouble.

An urgent need to push on made me hesitate when I started to unsaddle Vision. But I knew things could get worse. If they picked up my trail or spotted me, I'd have to ask Vision to give me his all. I had to let him rest and graze while he could.

"They may catch us," I told Prophet, thinking of the monster helicopter with its invasive splash of light interrupting the safety of the night. "But they've got it to do."

I decided to tie Vision to a low branch with enough rope to graze. I'd have to move him every hour. Hobbles could be dangerous. He might wander out into the open.

Pulling jerky from my saddlebag, I handed a piece to Prophet. "Breakfast," I said. "Then sleep."

I sat on the ground and chewed the nourishing meat then ate a handful of dried fruit. I thought of all the nights just six months before, when I'd stuffed myself with soda, chips, and candy in front of the TV. The nights of misery, when I was bored and restless, looking for something to fill my soul. The nights before I'd met Jacob on the river.

"Your body is sacred," he said, the day he put me on the rigorous diet and exercise plan. Then he showed me the poke greens that grew wild and told me how many vitamins it contained. "The People used to live on greens and fish and berries."

In the soft, morning light, I searched the dense under-growth and smiled when I saw the poke growing near the river. I knelt, picked the tender leaves and munched, think-ing of the sense of strength I had regained when the pounds dropped and lean muscle replaced soft flesh. After that, I would sometimes admire my naked body in front of a mirror and thank Jacob.

Moving Vision to a new spot with more grass, I retied him and rubbed his neck. Prophet whined and waited patiently as I unrolled my sleeping bag.

With Prophet warm against my neck I tried to sleep, but my eyes were wide open. I knew the fence problem was solved only temporarily. There would be more fences ahead. Other private tracts of land fenced down to the rivers' edge that would force us up into the open and around.

"Don't borrow trouble," I said, thinking of Pa Pa's favorite saying.

I forced myself to concentrate on the sound of the river. I thought about all of the afternoons alone with Jacob on the river. The two of us used to sit for hours by our small fire, listening to the peaceful journey of the river.

VII

The blast from the helicopter sent me crawling toward Vision. I grabbed his halter with one hand and commanded Prophet 'down' with the other.

Trees ripped overhead and for a horrible moment, the copter dipped so low I knew it would land. My heart thumped in my throat and my mind raced. If it landed, I'd have to leave everything, jump on Vision and disappear into the brush.

After the scare, I sat stroking Vision's neck and trembling. I untied him and led him toward the river. Dipping mud into the palm of both hands, I began to smear the dark slime over his light body. He nickered and moved his feet nervously.

"It's OK, boy. We have to camouflage you." I finished the task and allowed him to graze, dragging the halter rope.

"You're next," I told Prophet. Scooping up mud, I smeared his white cape and the snip on his face until it blended dark with the rest of his body.

I rubbed the mud on my face and hands, then began to

break camp and pack to ride. It amazed me that I'd slept most of the day. The sun was already leaning toward the western horizon.

"But this is good," I told Prophet. "We're probably safer at night."

Riding Vision in the cool quietness, I began to think of life and destiny and the possibility of a Higher Power.

"Do you believe in God?" I had asked Mom one evening over supper. It was just after we'd moved to the outskirts of Tulsa, when I was struggling with the memory of Wichita. I desperately needed a connection to something The memory of walking to church, hand in hand with Grammy and Pa Pa inspired my question.

My mother squirmed uncomfortably. "Not exactly," she admitted. "I'm what you'd call an agnostic."

"What does that mean?"

"It's complicated, CJ. I believe we are pretty much the captains of our own souls."

I'd left the room feeling really depressed. The idea of church seemed stupid to me after what Mom said. I felt as if I were just a little kid wandering around, desperate for someone to look after me.

I fired the same question to my dad a few weeks later.

"Of course, I believe in God," he said without hesitation.

"Why don't we go to church sometime?" I asked, thinking I might get close enough to Dad to confide in him about my problems.

Dad shifted his weight in his chair and picked up his paper from the end table. "Well, I've never been too much on organized religion."

"What's that mean?"

"It's complicated."

The sunset in front of me lit up the western sky with a brilliant splash of red-orange clouds tinged around the edges with white, as if an angry artist had thrown the three colors of paint against a slate blue canvas.

I pulled Vision to a halt and stared at the beauty.

"If you ever doubt God, just look around," Pa Pa had said. "Look at the trees and sunsets, the flowers, the joy in children's faces. It's not that complicated, CJ."

Nudging Vision back into a slow walk, I thought about the innocent years, before the divorce, when I had a natural faith.

My jaw tightened when I recalled the exact moment of my fall from grace. I was in Wichita at the new school, sitting alone in the cafeteria. *Maybe there isn't a God. Maybe we're just here then we die and its over and it doesn't matter one whit what we do or don't do.*

It was then I made the choice that changed my life. I stood and walked outside the building straight to the end of the school grounds where the Rebels were smoking.

"Looky here," Pepper said. "White girl thinks she can just come strollin up here and be one of us. Well, it ain't that easy, White Girl. There's a price to pay."

The memory of the words sent a shudder down my back and my fingers gripped the reins. I pulled Vision up and dismounted.

I thought about all the months of misery that one bad decision cost me. Then I remembered a time after Wichita when I felt close to God.

The morning I discovered my special feelings for

Jacob, I left the river and walked for miles. Everything seemed brighter and I was certain, if I held out my arms, I could fly up through the gold-red leaves of autumn and disappear into the sweetness of some glorious mystery. I realized it was Sunday when I heard the church bells ringing.

I walked straight into the nearby church with the joy of reunion burning my cheeks. I listened to every word the preacher said. Digested each syllable and nodded in complete agreement. When the song of invitation started, I went forward. On my knees, in front of a group of complete strangers, I humbly confessed for Wichita and asked forgiveness. Then I thanked God for His love and for the love I had for Jacob.

When moonlight began to filter through the trees, I realized I was at the shallow end of Keystone Lake. I began to strip off the saddle. Placing my gear in a heap under the trees, I took off my boots and clothes and led Vision out into the moonlight.

The quiet water looked like slate beneath the full moon. Vision whiffed it. I walked right out into the water and Vision followed. When he was up to his knees, he stopped and smelled again.

I took my hands and made easy waves, with a gentle motion. "Come, Prophet," I said. He splashed out from the bank, swimming toward us. I caught him in my arms. He felt warm against my neck and I held him. Then I released him in the water. He swam out, made a wide circle then went back toward the bank.

"See," I told Vision. "It's nothing to fear. It's fun. This is where you learn to swim, big guy. Just in case we have to cross the river."

Leading Vision back out of the water, I stopped him close to a fallen tree and mounted. He danced nervously for a moment.

"Probably never been ridden bareback," I said. "Well, you're gonna love this."

I took him back to the bank of the lake and let him stand with just his hooves in the soft mud. After a few minutes, I coaxed him forward, nudging with my heels. He took another step, then stopped.

"It's OK, buddy," I encouraged him, with a rub on the neck. I knew the bottom could fall out from under him at any second. Vision might feel a moment of panic. I had to be ready, keep astride him and cling to his mane. If I lost my balance and went off of his back, he might hurt me in his struggle to swim.

Another step, a pause, some encouragement. With his nose he began to splash playfully in the water and I laughed. The time was right. He wasn't afraid. I dug my bare heels into his flank, startling him. He lunged forward and we both went under. He came up blowing and I struggled to stay astride, to cling to his mane.

He swam straight out, toward the opposite bank, more than fifty yards away. A natural high quickly replaced my initial burst of fear. My pony swam with an even, confident stride, strongly pushing the water beneath him.

Prophet was barking from the bank. "Come on, boy," I yelled. I heard a splash and before Vision climbed the bank on the other side, Prophet came up on our left, passed us and was shaking in the cattails.

Vision lunged up through the boggy mud and stood, his legs quaking. "Good boy, good boy," I said, slapping his neck. "You're a natural born swimmer."

I rode him up into the dry grass and allowed him to graze and relax, while I sat on his back naked. I smiled to myself, filled with a new confidence.

"Let them try to catch us now." I whispered into the darkness. My body shivered in the coolness, but inside I had a warmth born of power and independence.

After a good rest, I turned Vision back to the lake's edge. I knew the real test lay ahead. Would he, after having his first experience of swimming, go into the lake again? It all depended on his heart.

"It's not the size of the horse," Pa Pa always said. "It's the size of his heart that matters."

"How big is your heart, little man?" I asked, making Vision step back into the water. Before I could even prod him with my feet, he was swimming. This time he didn't take either of us all the way under, but instead began to move through the water quickly when he first felt the ground go out from under him.

Prophet didn't wait for an invitation either. He was beside us. We moved easily through the quiet water like a sea monster frolicking in the privacy of the night.

"You have a heart as big as Texas," I told Vision when we reached the place in the trees where I'd dropped the saddle. And I knew, when he pushed his nose up into my arm for affection, I'd done what I promised myself I'd never do again. I'd fallen in love with another horse.

"I'll never put you through a sale ring. I don't care what happens. They can chase us forever. I won't give you or Prophet up." I made the oath standing naked and dripping in the moonlight.

"We'll stay here," I told Vision, rubbing his white again with mud then hobbling him. He stuck his head into the deep grass and began to tear at it.

Slipping back into my clothes, I longed for a small fire to heat one of my cans of beans, but I decided against it. The helicopter could come over at any moment. I wasn't certain they could spot the smoke in their light, but I couldn't take the chance.

I thought of the old man at the store. 'Haven't I seen you somewhere before?' If he made the connection, he'd have called the cops by now. If he'd done that, they could be swarming the highway not three miles away.

I opened one of the cans of cold beans and dived into them. They tasted better than anything I'd ever eaten. I thought about the swim in the darkness.

"Vision took to the water like a fish," I told Prophet. "We're ready for them now."

I put Vision on a long line and tied the rope to a low hanging branch, then settled into my sleeping bag.

My belly full and my mind at peace about the river, I drifted quickly to sleep. I was swimming the muddy river and people were chasing me. Bank to bank Vision swam and I screamed at Prophet to follow, but the people were getting closer and closer.

Climbing up on the bank, drenched and shaking from the cold water, I heard someone up ahead. My body was exhausted and Vision was stumbling beneath me. Prophet looked lank and hungry and my own belly churned with emptiness.

My grandfather appeared in the distance, barely visible in the trees. I gasped when I first saw him because of the circle of white light surrounding him. He turned and began to walk away.

"Pa Pa!" I screamed. "Wait, I want to come with you."

"You will make it home, CJ," Pa Pa said, then the light around him burst into a thousand golden birds that flew away.

I sat up abruptly faced with the silence of the night. I thought of the dream detail by detail and it left me in awe. My grandfather's spirit was not dead. The thought made me gather Prophet in my arms and stare up at the stars.

It was the first time in three years I'd been that close to him, been able to actually see his face, hear his voice.

The memory gave me such a sweet sense of peace, I thought again about the little church and how my connection to God had grown since that day. I still didn't understand a lot, but I knew good and evil existed. I toyed with evil in Wichita. It had almost destroyed me. After that, I had a new respect for God.

I put my hands together staring up at the night sky, but words wouldn't form on my lips. *Jacob is gone.* The thought replaced my earlier sense of peace with boiling turmoil.

Prophet tensed in my embrace and pulled away. His ears perked and he looked down river and whined. I thought I heard something in the far distance. Straining my ears to connect to the vague sound I sat, waiting for it to come again.

A faint bellow, a kind of moaning howl did come again. It caused my breath to catch in my throat. Bloodhounds! My heart pounded with a dull thud.

Behind me, miles to the east, I could hear dogs. People were after me on foot with dogs. They must have started tracking near the river by Jacob's tee-pee where Drake and the sheriff had seen me. They were probably near our first night's camp. Probably found my fire. The hounds would take over from there. Between me, Vision and Prophet, we would leave a scent even an inexperienced dog could easily follow.

I pictured trained bloodhounds lunging forward, crashing through the trees with an army of eager cops behind them.

"Things have changed," I said, jumping out of my sleeping bag. "We'll be riding more and resting less."

The first traces of early light were coloring the eastern sky. "Sorry it was a short rest," I told Vision, plopping the saddle in place and beginning to cinch it. "We have to move now."

I knew the only way to throw the dogs off our scent would be to cross the river. As I led Vision toward the frothing water, I also knew the risks of the river were many. It wouldn't be the peaceful, nighttime swim in a calm lake with no saddle and gear. I checked everything and double tied my saddle bags. My backpack could get me in trouble. If the current caught it just right, it might very well pull me off Vision and slam me down stream.

I carefully selected the things from the pack I would

need most. I strapped the filet knife to my gun belt, shoved my notebook and pen into a plastic bag and crammed it into my saddle bag next to the fishing gear.

Holding the backpack, I said good-bye to my coffee pot, can opener, fork, knife, plate and cup. I tried stuffing the flashlight into saddle bags but it wouldn't go. I held it in my hand for a few minutes, staring. It was heavy and I could do without it. I had matches and a cigarette lighter that would have to do. I shoved the flashlight into the backpack and zipped the pack quickly, casting all worry from my mind. If I got in trouble in the current, I'd release the backpack and let it disappear into the darkness of the muddy water.

With calm resolve I began to walk, leading Vision, considering each bend along the river. In some places, the bank wasn't steep, but just below would be a tangle of fallen logs or debris. The river might sweep us into the tangle and if Vision wasn't strong enough to fight the current, he could drown.

As I walked and looked, Prophet began to whine. His ears could hear the hounds better than mine. I only caught a faint echo of the baying every few minutes, but I knew my dog could hear them steadily progressing toward us, gaining. I saw it in his worried eyes, the way he kept stopping to look back.

"There is no perfect spot," I finally told myself, putting my foot in the stirrup.

I looked down at the river. It was wide and wild, but clear of debris. The bank on the other side looked steep. I walked Vision into the water. He snorted but didn't resist. We stood for a moment, while the water lapped up around his knees. Prophet didn't wait. He bailed into the river and began to swim. His light body was immediately carried down stream with the current. I nudged Vision forward and he plunged in.

The force of water slapped us down stream like the blow from a giant's hand. I clung to Vision's mane and tried to keep my legs on either side of his back, but the current yanked us to the left. The back pack pulled me under. I closed my eyes and fought my way up, spitting water. Letting go of the mane with my right hand, I slipped my shoulder from the bag and with a shove, sent it bobbing off.

My head came up and I blinked back the water, desperately holding on against the ripping current. Vision floundered once, went below the surface and came up blowing and snorting. I prayed he wouldn't panic and try to turn back.

"Go boy!" I screamed above the roar of the water, "Swim."

He seemed smart enough to know there was no turning back. He reached out and fought the angry current, determined to reach the distant bank. I tried to look off to my left to see if we were heading for trouble, to try to spot Prophet, but could see nothing but boiling muddy water.

Half-way across, I saw the snakes. Water moccasins, relaxing in the current, with their heads above the surface. I thought of my pistol strapped securely to my waist, but it was impossible. If I turned loose with one hand I'd be stripped off of Vision in seconds. I clung tighter, closed my eyes and prayed.

Then I felt Vision's feet scrambling and opened my eyes

to the glorious bank of sand stretched out warm and golden in the afternoon sun. Vision climbed out on the sand and shook and I laughed when Prophet came running from the brush.

"We did it! I screamed. "Saddle and almost all of our gear." I dismounted and checked my saddle bags.

But, rubbing Vision's neck, I realized it would be asking too much for him to swim the river twice in one day. Lowering his neck, he put his nose to the warm sand and snorted. He wanted to roll, so I quickly stripped the saddle and tossed it aside.

Vision went down on his front knees and gave a grunt as his body hit the ground. He rolled in the clean, warm sand, rubbing his back and neck into the softness. After he stood and shook, he pushed his nose into the crook of my arm.

"You did good, buddy. Real good," I said, but our moment of affection was interrupted by the blast of a helicopter.

I grabbed the saddle and tried running, leading Vision, but I didn't get out of sight in time. The giant hovered over me as I disappeared into the trees. I could almost hear him on the radio. "We've spotted her. She's on the north bank of the Arkansas River south east of . . . "

My intentions had been to rest and allow my pony to graze, but now that was impossible. I brushed sand from Vision's wet belly and tightened the cinch. Cops would be swarming soon. Our swim across the river to escape the dogs was for nothing. Now they'd be coming at me from both sides.

I mounted and sat in the wet saddle, my hair still dripping. Thoughts darted through my mind. *Which way should I go? It's a crap shoot. I will need a lot of luck to slip by them now.*

Another nagging fear surfaced. The helicopter seemed to be locating me with ease. I'd heard somewhere about an infra-red sensor, the latest technology. I knew little about it, but if they used that to track me, the security of the trees probably meant nothing. I also knew, if they found a place to set the copter down, I could be surrounded within minutes.

A shadow of clouds made me squint toward the sky, and what I saw made my lips stretch into a smile. Heavy, dark clouds boiled on the horizon and the mid-day sun began to evaporate into a stagnate yellow soup.

"Maybe it isn't over," I said, patting Vision's neck. "A bad storm will play havoc with their helicopter and hounds."

I made a quick decision to circle back east in an attempt to throw them off. Reining Vision around, I started him in an easy walk. His plodding pace told me he was tired from the swim. I had to let him conserve his energy.

It started to rain slowly and the wind whistled through the trees. Hunger gnawed at me and I shook from the cold. Thunder boomed in the distance and lightning streaked across the late afternoon sky. I pulled Vision up and untied my slicker from behind the saddle. It was drenched, like my clothes and boots, but it would help hold my body heat closer.

Rummaging in the saddle bag, I pulled out the soggy crackers and left them on the ground for the birds. I threw Prophet a piece of jerky and took the last piece in my hand. Except for the one can of beans, my food was gone.

It poured and the mass of dark clouds engulfed us like a fog. I kept riding, determined to go as far as I could.

The wind blasted through the trees, causing limbs to crash down in our path. Streaks of light snapped and buzzed all around us. I knew how dangerous lightning was around horses and I began to get nervous, so I dismounted and led Vision. The roar became so intense, I was sure a tornado was in the making.

"Prophet, are you with us?" I screamed every so often. His shrill bark would slice through the storm and fill me with security. I began to talk back to him.

"One thing about it, boy, they'll never find us in this." I had less fear of the storm than the search party. As I bent forward and walked, I entertained myself with thoughts of a tornado whisking the three of us into an Oz-like land where Jacob and Pa Pa would greet me.

The wet dimness turned into black night and the storm raged. Vision told me every few steps he'd had enough by stopping and putting his head down to protect himself against the pounding rain.

I began to look for some kind of shelter to protect my animals from the growing fury. I remembered Pa Pa's advice about tornados. 'Find a hole, a place beneath the ground level, a cave, anything and get out from under the trees.'

Not more than fifty feet away, I saw an overhang and stared for a moment in disbelief. When I walked forward I half expected the dark hole to be a mirage I'd created out of my desperation.

Feeling before me with my hands, I shouted out in

excitement. "We're safe!" As I led Vision in to the quiet dryness of the cave, he nickered and shook the drenching wetness from his body. Prophet did the same thing at the exact same time.

The overhang was huge, deep and roomy. I walked the length of it in the darkness and wished for my flashlight. "A fire," I said, "they'll never see smoke in this storm."

I pulled the sopping saddle off of Vision's back, then fumbled through my saddle bags for the plastic baggie that held my box of matches. When my hands finally felt the treasure, I let out a sigh. I struck a match and tried to hold it in the safety of my palm, but the wind quickly snuffed it out.

Feeling once again in the saddlebags, I finally came upon the cigarette lighter. I flicked it several times before it lit, then cupped my hands around the flame.

Dry driftwood lay scattered along the floor of the cave. I crawled along, gathering small twigs into a pile. Inching my way back to the saddle, I felt inside the bag for my notebook in the safety of its plastic bag. I tore some pages from the back and crawled back to the broken twigs.

A few minutes later I had a small fire blazing. I searched impatiently for the remaining can of beans. I held the lighter close to my saddle and stared. One side of the saddle bags had come open. The beans were gone.

My teeth chattered and my belly growled. For one horrible moment, fear paralyzed me and I hovered closer and closer over my fire. Then I pushed my shaking body up and forced myself into action. Breaking limbs, I piled them waist high until the fire roared. If I couldn't warm myself on the inside, I'd make sure the outside was warm.

I made a makeshift rack tepee, by tying a circle of the driftwood limbs together at the top with a piece of rope. Placing it near the fire, I took off my clothes and draped them around to dry. Vision's saddle blanket went on the rack and my change of clothes from the saddle bags.

As I hovered close to the fire I decided hot water would warm me and I could do fine on that until morning. My mind went immediately to the river. I knew instantly I'd made another big mistake. I'd sent the coffee pot downstream in the backpack. I grabbed my canteen and shook it. I had a few swallows of water, but no way to warm it.

I opened the canteen and placed it under the eave of the cave. Water ran in a steady trickle. Seconds later, I drank long swallows of the cool wetness and some of my confidence returned.

The rain raged, lightning cracked and thunder vibrated the roof of the cave. Vision needed to graze, but I couldn't chance letting him out in the storm. Prophet looked at me and I saw hunger and worry in his eyes.

"I have no idea what to do. I've made so many mistakes," I said to Prophet.

Vision quests are done at times of great personal doubt. Jacob's words came clearly to my mind. *The Sioux would go to a secluded place and stay for days and nights without food. They would search for answers with the eyes of their hearts.*

VIII

I meditated through the night. The rain was still falling the next morning and I moved only to hobble Vision, knowing his hunger would soon lure him out into the storm.

Prophet left and returned. I heard the crunch of bones and relaxed, knowing he was fed. My own hunger began to wane as the hours passed.

Images danced across my mind and I let them come and go with a heart open to guidance. The shooting played out in slow motion with crystal clear images of things I hadn't remembered before.

"Run! run!" the scream came through the hallway as I sat in study hall cramming for my Algebra exam. Then I heard the shots that echoed like a cannon down the empty halls.

"He's in the gym! He has a gun!"

The substitute teacher looked up. Everyone looked at each other with question. Kids began to flood out of classrooms across the hall and I could hear the big double doors banging as people fled from the school.

Someone grabbed my hand and jerked me to my feet. I stared at her moving lips but couldn't seem to hear her words. Then she pushed me out the door and I became part of the stampede that dashed into the school yards. I was looking for Jacob, wanting to run back and make sure he was safe.

In the semi-darkness of the cave, I stood and began to move around my fire chanting. "Hey, hey, hey, yah, hey." I let the words come from a hurting place deep in my soul. I danced the way Jacob danced when we were alone on the river.

When I slumped back into a sitting position, weak and exhausted, Jacob came to the cave. He brought me hot soup and dry clothes. He took warm oil, made me stretch out on a buffalo robe and massaged the aching weariness from my body.

"I love you, CJ." His voice was liquid with emotion and his green eyes sparked with passion.

"I love you, too," I said, touching his face. "I'm sorry I didn't say it before."

"We have to go back, you know. To Fremont."

"Jacob, let's not go back. Let's ride free, the two of us, forever."

His gentle hands turned suddenly rough. Jacob was no longer with me. This boy had dark, greasy hair and brown eyes, his teeth were dirty and he reeked of alcohol.

"No," I said. "I don't want to. No!"

Something in the distance cried out a warning. I couldn't quite grasp the reality, but the sound came again.

"Keeeeer. Keeeeer. Keeeeer."

It took me several minutes to realize where I was. I shivered and drew my bare legs up to my chest. The fire was out and the rain had stopped.

The cry came again, closer.

"Keeeeer."

A red-tailed hawk sat just outside on a low branch of a cottonwood.

"Keeeeer!" the cry had alarm in it. "Run!"

Prophet growled.

I heard voices and froze for a horrible second, then jumped up and slid quickly into my stiff clothes. I pulled on my boots and grabbed my halter rope, leaping out through the sopping grass and dripping trees toward Vision.

Two men, standing with fishing poles, stared.

"Look, it's that girl. The one everyone's looking for." The voice came, crystal clear across the crisp afternoon stillness. "There's a huge reward," the other said, "let's get her."

My hands trembled as I fumbled with the hobbles. I only had time to unbuckle one side. No time for a saddle, no time to return to the cave and get my precious notebook and belongings. With the halter rope, I twisted a quick slip knot over Vision's nose and led him to a stump. As I jumped on his back and dug my heels into his sides, I heard the men running up.

"Grab her!" One of them was beside me. I felt his huge hand brush past my knee as Vision leaped forward.

They ran after me. Prophet raced in front and Vision half ran, half hopped as the hobbles banged against his free leg. For more than an hour, they pursued us. Once, when Vision slowed to circle a fallen log, I heard footsteps thudding through the mud and a curse echoed as we disappeared.

Finally, I stopped Vision and sat for a long time, listening. When I was sure we'd lost the men, I dismounted and unbuckled the hobbles, running my hands up and down Vision's muddy leg where the heavy strap left welts of swollen flesh.

"I'm sorry, buddy," I said, putting my arms around his neck. I knelt and took Prophet in my arms. My body trembled from the rush of adrenalin that had drained my remaining strength.

"We have to keep moving." I mounted Vision and let him travel at his own pace, first running, then trotting, slowing to a walk and picking his way through the fallen debris from the storm. I encouraged him on and on until we were well out of range of the men on foot.

When I pulled Vision up, I thought for a minute about my precious belongings. The two men would rummage through them. Take my saddle, Bandit's saddle and bridle. The pistol Pa Pa gave me. The box Jacob made. They'd probably read my journal.

A helicopter roared just over head, paused, then continued down river. Before the roar had left my ears, I heard the distinct baying of hounds. Prophet's ears perked and the hair stood up on the back of his neck.

"Keeeer." The cry quieted my fears. I looked up, squinting against the sun, searching until I caught sight of the dark speck in the clear sky.

I didn't understand the significance of the hawk, but I

felt certain he was what Jacob would call my spirit guide. I would trust his guidance. This time his call did not radiate alarm. It simply said, "Follow me."

I held Vision to a walk, encouraging him to relax not knowing what was ahead. The barking hounds grew nearer. The helicopter buzzed closer and closer, but the hawk continued and so did I.

Pausing at the river's edge, I allowed Vision and Prophet to drink. I felt dryness pulling at my own throat, but I had no canteen, no fresh water.

A noise behind us startled Vision and he jumped forward, going to his knees in the swirling water. Prophet growled. When I turned, I saw an army of cops approaching, dozens of them, all with rifles, all running toward me.

"Get down off of your horse and put your hands over your head," a voice boomed. The fat sheriff had not given up. His broad face appeared through the trees wearing a smirk of satisfaction. "Thought I couldn't catch you, huh?"

"You haven't caught me . . . yet."

I dug my heels into Vision's flanks and yelled. He hit the water with a splash, knowing what he had to do. The swirling water came up over my head and I surfaced, grabbing for mane, struggling to stay astride, but the current slammed us violently down stream and my body was first on one side of Vision, then the other. I felt my hands sliding down the golden mane and I scrambled to cling to my life line with every fiber of strength left in my body. My gelding floundered, paddled, and kept his wide eyes on the opposite bank.

"Look at that," a voice screamed out over the water.

"She's swimming the damned river."

"Damn, crazy little witch," the sheriff replied.

The vicious, rain-swollen river continued to sweep us down, as Vision struggled forward and I held on with both hands, the current slamming my body around like a rubber raft in the rapids. I closed my eyes against the sting of the muddy water. When I opened them, I saw a waterlogged tree coming on the current to my left. It rumbled behind us, moving like a whale in the water, missing Vision's rump by inches. I clung to Vision and urged him on, saying a quick prayer for Prophet who had been swept away down stream.

Vision's feet began to flounder against something, and he pulled himself forward in sticky, bogging mud. We smacked our way up through the sludge and out of the flooding river.

I'd barely begun to slow my breathing and Vision's legs were still quaking beneath him when I heard voices again.

"There she is!" came the cry, and again I was amazed at the army of men approaching me through the trees. I reached and patted Vision's neck. I knew trying to go back in the river would be suicide for us both.

"Prophet!" I screamed, but my dog was not in sight.

Squeezing my heels into Vision's side easily, I asked him for whatever he had left. The gelding's head flipped up and he took off in a soft gallop. We approached a clearing that led to the highway. I stopped dead still and stared in horror. The road, for as far as I could see, was lined with cop cars.

A voice came across the field over some kind of speaker,

"Connie Jean McGee, get off of your horse and put your face on the ground. You are surrounded."

The hawk flew directly toward them, hovered over them. "Tokhe shni." The words came into my mind in Jacob's Indian accent and brought a savage calm to my racing heart.

Prophet barked and I saw him running toward me. I dived off of Vision and grabbed the soggy dog, kissing him as he whined in pleasure at the reunion.

Something brushed my arm and I stared. Purple pokeberries plumping in the warm sun beckoned to me.

The dogs and men approached behind me. The army of troops up ahead waited, repeating orders over the speaker. The hawk continued to urge me forward.

"Keeeeer, Keeeeer, Keeeeer."

I took a handful of the berries and squeezed them into purple pulp in my hand. I marked a jagged line across the white half of Prophet's nose, turned to Vision and did the same to his neck. I streaked both of my cheeks and my forehead.

Slinging myself up on Vision with a burst of strength that surprised me, I approached the clearing, paused, and rubbed Vision's neck.

"You've been a fine friend. I love you." Looking down at Prophet I said, "That goes for you too."

I dug my heels into Vision's flanks and he surged out into the broad brightness of the afternoon sun, running straight toward the mass of shining badges, guns and cars in front of us.

"We will ride free, Jacob," I whispered into the wind.

"We will ride free."

I screamed out an Indian war cry and leaned forward, close to Vision's neck. Shots rang out and stirred dust as they hit the ground near me. I pushed on, harder, straight toward the long line of police.

Vision's legs gave way beneath me and I tumbled forward hitting the ground and rolling. My pony kicked and moaned. Struggling back to his feet, he scrambled several steps, then fell. I could see his golden mane blowing in the Oklahoma wind and I reached for it. Where was Prophet? I tried to turn my head but couldn't move.

The red-tailed hawk loomed above me and I focused on him as he faded, faded into the cloudless, blue sky.

"Keeeer, Keeeeer, Keeeeer."

IX

She's awake, sir." The voice registered in my head before
I opened my eyes. I blinked several times trying to
focus on my surroundings. I was in a hospital bed with
tubes connected to my right wrist and a brace tight against
my neck. The first thought that came to mind was of Vision
and Prophet. Had they shot my pony and dog?

I started to move my arm and something clanged, metal
against metal. My left arm was handcuffed to the bed rail!
When I tried to turn my head, pain shot up my back and I
let out a low moan.

"She's awake, sir," the voice repeated, farther from me.

I heard a door open, footsteps squeaked across the
waxed floor, then a tall man with piercing eyes towered
over me.

"Connie Jean McGee?" The question boomed out into
the quietness of the room. Three more men walked in, one
carrying a tape recorder.

"You have the right to remain silent. You have . . . "

He read my rights as I stared straight ahead at the ceiling, then he began to fire questions at me as fast as he could talk.

"Where were you on the morning of . . .during the shooting at Fremont High? Did you know a boy named Jacob Johnson? Why did you run away from home?"

He kept on and on, firing the questions at me, the wrinkles in his dark brow growing more ominous, his voice impatient.

"Tokhe shni," I said, in a low curse.

The man stared at me with a perplexed expression as a nurse walked in and began checking my pulse and taking my temperature.

"When can she be released?" the detective barked. "We need her down at the station." He gave me a despicable look. "You'll talk, young lady. Before it's over, you'll talk." Turning to the nurse, he repeated the question, "When can she be released?"

The nurse turned intense brown eyes on the detective. "That's up to the doctor. She's suffering from hypothermia, she's dehydrated and has several pulled muscles in her neck and back. The more rest she gets, the sooner she'll be released."

Mom crashed into the room, marched over to the detective and got in his face. "Get out of here at once. My lawyer is on his way up and you have no right to be badgering CJ when she first opens her eyes."

I had to struggle to hold back a smile. *Get em Maggie.* The detective gave my mom an impatient glance. "You would be her mother, I presume."

"You'd presume right." Mom walked to my side and

squeezed my hand, smoothing my kinky, tangled hair away from my forehead. "She's been through enough. Being ATTACKED by a damned army and having her horse shot out from under her. How many grown men does it take to catch one frightened fifteen year old girl?"

"Ma'am the FBI has been called in. You have to know this is a serious matter. Your daughter had connections to . . . "

A little man in a three-piece suit walked into the room. Although he was small, he commanded a certain respect that brought a lingering silence.

"Ron," the detective nodded.

The lawyer looked up at the detective with a piercing glance. "Shame on you. Already here harassing my client."

"She hasn't said anything." The authority in the tall cop's voice dwindled to a tone of dread. "Well, she said something, but I have no idea what. It was some kind of gibberish."

"Lucky for you." The lawyer didn't take his eyes off the detective. "Now if I could have a word with my client in private."

The detective and cops slowly filed out of the room just as Dad came in. He took three giant strides toward me and stared. I could tell he wanted to hug me, but thought it impossible with all of my attachments.

"Sweetheart, I've been so worried. Are you OK? Everything will be all right."

"That remains to be seen," Mom said, staring at Dad with a new level of hatred.

"Don't start," Dad said to her through gritted teeth.

The words made me stiffen against the sheets and I

stared straight up to the ceiling. Now they were both blaming each other for me running away. I closed my eyes and thought of Vision and Prophet and saw myself riding along the river.

"C J." Mom was over me, shaking me gently. "This is Mr. Graves. He needs to ask you some questions, honey. Do you feel like talking?"

I blinked my eyes back open and stared at Mom. Part of me wanted to talk. Wanted to ask about Vision. Had they killed my pony? Where was Prophet? I wanted to beg them to take care of my animals. But I knew neither of them had time for such things and they meant nothing to them.

"She probably just needs to rest," Dad said, as he grabbed my left hand and saw the handcuffs. "God. Is this necessary, Graves?"

The lawyer was looking at me intently. I held his gaze for a moment and saw many things. Compassion, understanding, and a strong sense of self-confidence.

"There are certain things we have little control over," the lawyer said. "The sooner CJ talks to us the faster we can get her home."

"HOME?" I wanted to shout. Home for me is along the river with Vision and Prophet. But I looked away from him and back toward the ceiling.

Dad held tight to one hand and Mom to the other, as if they'd be happy if only they could split me asunder.

"Connie Jean, honey. No matter what you've done, how . . . bad it is," Dad said, "I'm with you. You have to tell Mr. Graves the truth. Everything. It's the only way he can help you."

Dad's concern was evident in the dark circles beneath his eyes. A part of me wanted to tell him how I had known Jacob for months. How kind and caring and good he was to me. But just as the words started to form in my mouth and I drummed up the courage to speak, Dad attacked Mom.

"If you'd kept better track of where she was," he spit. "How could she have been hanging around with this boy and you never ever saw him, Maggie? How?"

Mom's eyes sparked with fiery anger. "I have to work, remember. CJ is nearly an adult. I don't follow her around like she's a toddler. You have a lot of damned nerve, blaming me for this, you son of a bitch."

"So it's my fault?"

"Kids," the lawyer said in a soft voice. There was a hint of amusement in his expression. "Kids, this won't help."

My parents were worse than ever. I squinted at them, "Tokhe shni." I said the words with impatient passion.

"I think she's pissed," the lawyer said, his dark eyebrows raised in a high arch above the blue eyes. "Wonder why?"

Mom and Dad looked at him.

"Maybe the two of you should . . . continue your discussion out in the hall. Leave us alone for awhile."

My parents looked hurt and confused, and left reluctantly.

I liked the small man, his calm manner, the way he seemed to understand me even though I hadn't said a word.

A chair squeaked on the tile floor as the lawyer sat next to my bed and crossed his legs. He was below me, and I kept my eyes on the ceiling.

"They are charging you with eleven counts of first degree murder in the Fremont school shooting." His words caused a shock of goose bumps to travel down my legs beneath the starched sheets.

"Because of what a . . . " the lawyer thumbed through some papers in his hand, "Mr. Drake is saying, the authorities have proof you knew Jacob Johnson. Mr. Drake apparently saw you at his son's hideout along the Arkansas River. The dog, one Border Collie, was with you when you were apprehended." The voice stopped and I knew in the silence that followed the lawyer was searching for just the right words. I had the distinct feeling he understood my anger and had no intention of trying to berate me for anything. He was just trying to do his job.

"CJ. Is that what you like to be called?" He waited and when I didn't answer he continued. "The horror of the school shooting has caused national attention. The President of the U.S. is calling a special committee to examine the causes of this atrocity and try to find answers. Since the shooter, Jacob Johnson, isn't around to blame, these detectives are looking for a scapegoat. You are it." He let another long silence pass.

"Pretty much everything in life is a choice. If you choose not to talk to me or to them, I'm afraid you will go to jail. That's your decision. No one can keep that from happening. If you choose to talk to me, I'll do everything I can to help."

The next silence was so long, I thought he was just going to sit for hours until I said something. Finally the chair squeaked against the clean floor and he stood, looking down at me.

"I . . . can see why you're angry." He cast a wary glance toward the hall where my parents' voices rattled on and on. "I wish I could offer you some profound advice on the subject, but I have none. If you decide to talk to me, I'll be back. In the meantime, I'll do everything I can to keep you out of jail tomorrow. But . . . it doesn't look too good."

Seconds after the lawyer walked out, the detectives, cops, and my parents returned. I heard Mom's voice, commanding me, pressuring me to speak to her, the emotion in Dad's voice as he pleaded, and the detective's stern warning about what the next day was going to bring if I didn't talk.

I shut all of it out. Closing my eyes, I put myself on Vision swimming the river. I could feel his power pulling me forward as the muddy water whipped my body from side to side. I thought of Prophet nuzzled next to my neck as we cuddled beneath the stars. I thought of my vision quest and my guide, the red-tailed hawk.

But why did the hawk lead me back to this?

Angry voices pulled me into the sterile surroundings of the hospital room. Even before I opened my eyes, I could feel the hate radiating across me from Mom to Dad.

"Tokhe shni," I said with no emotion, staring straight up at the ceiling.

I finally closed my eyes again in an attempt to connect to the peacefulness of the light that had surrounded Pa Pa in my dream. I wanted in the worst way to ask about Vision, to tell my parents to take care of Prophet. But their animosity toward each other stopped me cold. I didn't care if I ever spoke to either of them again.

129

Drifting into a troubled sleep, I was once again near the river riding Vision, and Prophet was with me. A loud 'Keeeeer' shattered the peaceful moment and then I was alone, running, calling for Prophet, searching for Vision. I looked in the sky for the hawk, but he wasn't there. Everything seemed empty, as if I were the only one left alive in the universe, and the fear of loneliness swallowed me up as I began to panic.

Gunshots burst around me, kids screaming and running. I was standing back in the school yard at Fremont High and I heard the girl utter the words that would forever be etched into my soul.

"I don't think he goes to school at Fremont. I've never seen him before . . . but he's shooting people. Shooting them . . . He had these feathers hanging from his hair and his face was painted."

"No!" I screamed, "No Jacob."

I awoke in a damp shuffle of sheets surrounded by the same roomful of people, all of them staring at me with horror in their eyes.

Mom was the first to speak. She cleared her throat, her eyes still wide with shock. "CJ, I demand that you talk to me this minute. Tell us everything you know about this boy, Jacob."

I knew then what I'd done. I'd shouted Jacob's name to the room full of cops, to the tall detective, to my parents.

Struggling up with my elbows, I winced when the pulled muscles in my back pinched me with pain. Dad quickly helped me get comfortable and reached for my hand.

"Sweetheart, we can't help you if you won't talk."

I felt the room closing in on me. All the eyes fixed and

staring, the deathly silence, the pressure. Suddenly, none of it mattered. I just didn't care. They could do what they wanted with me, put me in jail, go on with their lives.

It would do no good to tell them anything, because they weren't going to believe me anyhow. If I spilled my guts, told them about how I met Jacob, how I saw him that first day alone on the river meditating, what a gentle spirit he was and how he'd saved me from myself, they would declare me insane.

A reporter somehow managed to get into the room, past the wall of security guards and the cops. She came blasting next to the bed, camera posed, and snapped a picture of me handcuffed to the bed.

In a rare display of temper, my father grabbed the camera and, cursing, threw it to the floor. "You get out of here or I swear . . . "

Then, through the maze of chatter and confusion, I heard someone else making her way toward my bed. People seemed to be clearing a path, moving aside to make way for this visitor.

Mrs. Mac snatched me up in her fat arms and with handcuffs rattling and tubes bouncing, she held me in her vice grip. The flood of grief I'd been holding back pressed heavily against my self-control, like a great dam starting to break beneath the pressure of a rain swollen river.

"Tokhe shni," I said, determined not to lose control of my emotions in front of the crowd. "Tokhe shni."

I was safe in those familiar, loving arms. I knew she was the one person left in the world who truly cared what happened to me.

X

With the authority only a teacher can have, Mrs. Mac cleared the room. "Leave us alone," she growled in a voice I'd seldom heard in her classroom.

Slowly, everyone filed out. Dad gave my hand a little squeeze. "Sweetheart . . . I'm willing to do anything, anything I can to help you through this." He looked at the stranger across from him.

"I don't know who you are. But thank you for caring about Connie Jean." He extended his hand. "I'm Alan McGee, Connie Jean's father."

"Mrs. Mac, high school English-Lit. Your daughter is a talented writer."

The news was a shock to Dad. He looked down at me and something painful came across his face. With watery eyes, he retreated toward the door.

Mrs. Mac grabbed me up one more time. She wasn't going to demand anything. She was genuinely glad to see that I was OK.

When she finally let go of me, she stood, smoothing the

hair from my face. "You've been through quite an ordeal. I've heard about those morons chasing you for days. Is there anything I can do?"

Words burned in my throat. *Please, please, find out about my pony, Vision. I think they shot him. He fell out from under me. That's the last thing I remember. And my dog, Prophet, if he's alive, I can't bear the thought of him sitting in some kennel wondering where I am. Please don't let them hurt Prophet.*

But the words wouldn't come to my lips. What was the point? Unless I ran away again, I couldn't keep my pony or my dog. If I didn't break my silence, maybe everyone would leave me alone. In jail at least I could be in peace.

Mrs. Mac held my free right hand in her two chubby paws. We both remained silent for a long while. Then she patted my cheek and smiled. "CJ, if you want to talk to me, I promise I won't tell them anything you don't want me to say. She raised her eyebrows and straightened her shoulders. "I'll go to jail first," she said, then chuckled.

I didn't smile, but it was good to be with another human being who loved me, someone I could trust. I struggled once again with the possibility of telling her everything, but the detectives, my parents, the lawyer and District Attorney would make her life miserable if she didn't tell them what I said.

"It does not matter what mistakes you've made here, if any." Mrs. Mac's broad forehead was creased with a frown. "I'll still love you no matter what."

I knew she meant it. I yearned to confide in Mrs. Mac about my journey. I had a passion to tell her I saw my grandfather in the light, about my vision quest and the red-tail.

But lying handcuffed to that bed, all of it seemed suddenly childish and I wondered if I'd dreamed it just to help me with the pain of losing Jacob.

"CJ, I know you and Jacob had feelings for one another, that you were friends."

I turned my head and looked right into Mrs. Mac's eyes behind the upside down glasses. How could she possibly know?

"I have an intuitive nature," my teacher admitted, still staring straight at me. "Many times in class I'd catch Jacob looking at you . . . tenderly, when you didn't know it."

Her words sent a rush of vibrating pain across my shoulders that radiated down my back clear to my toes.

"Tokhe shni," I said, gritting my teeth.

Jerking me up once again into her iron arms, Mrs. Mac ran her soft hands over my head, "There, there, now. It'll be OK."

The reality of her words was too painful, I had to shut them out. "Tokhe shni," I repeated, wanting her to leave."

"It's OK, baby. He knew you loved him. It'll all be OK."

I heard the door open and the scuffle of feet. I wiggled out of Mrs. Mac's arms and back into the sheets, eyes on the ceiling, just as the detectives and District Attorney appeared next to my bed. Mom's lawyer followed close behind.

"The doctor is releasing you tomorrow morning, Connie Jean," the detective informed me in his professional voice. "You'll be held in the county jail until the arraignment. You could make this a lot easier on yourself by talking to us." The man looked across the bed at Mrs. Mac.

"This is a criminal investigation, ma'am. Withholding evidence is a felony. If you don't cooperate with us, you could be subpoenaed."

"Yes," Mrs. Mac said, looking straight into the detective's face. "You can subpoena me, but you can't make me say what you need to hear." Then she looked down at me and winked. "I'll be back," she said, putting a spiral notebook and pen in my hands. "If you can't talk, maybe you could write."

Then she was gone and Mom was on one side of the bed with William. Cindy had joined Dad and stood with him on the other side.

The detective started in on me again. "Did you know Jacob Johnson? Did you have anything to do with his acquiring the gun? Where were you on the day of the shooting?"

"Tokhe shni," I said, looking straight in his eyes.

The lawyer got an amused look on his face and shrugged at the detective.

"Let me have some more time with my client alone," he said. The impeccably groomed lawyer again screeched the chair next to my bed. It seemed to me he thought he might get more out of me if I couldn't see him. He waited until the room was empty.

I kept thinking about Mrs. Mac's words. "Many times in class I'd catch Jacob Johnson looking at you . . . tenderly, when you didn't know it." I reached to rub the iron clamp of pain in my throat with my left hand, but succeeded only in rattling my handcuffs.

"CJ," the lawyer started then hesitated. "This shooting is a great tragedy. You probably know it's one of many school shootings that have shocked the nation over the past few years. All of us are desperate for answers. If you can shine any light on an answer, you could help a lot of people."

His words again hung in the silence of the room and I wrestled with the thoughts. Finally his chair slid back, he stood, looked at me, then smiled.

"You get some rest now. I'll try to call off the troops for this evening, but tomorrow could be grueling."

The door shut, then opened again as Mom, William, Dad and Cindy all came back in, taking their places on opposite sides of my bed, the Union and Confederate troops forming behind their lines, preparing for attack.

"The doctor is releasing you tomorrow, sweetheart." Dad was the first to reach for my hand. Mom immediately took my other hand. I prepared myself for the next battle in the five-year war.

"Our lawyer, Ron Graves, is the best in the state, in this part of the country," Mom said. "Tomorrow he will start the process to get you out on bail. But . . . it looks as if you will have to be held in jail a few days."

"He's doing everything he can to prevent that, Sweetheart," Dad continued. "But you have to talk to them. Tell them how you knew this boy. If you tell them everything, you'll be out of trouble and we can go home."

I cast my eyes toward Dad's new wife, who was biting on a hang nail and looking at me like, if she had three wishes, the first would be for me to disappear forever so she could have a life.

Turning, I deliberately looked into William's eyes, who stood stoic and rigid next to Mom. His expression showed similar wishes, with more animosity. I was the only thing standing between him and Mom. His money might not be running out, but his patience was.

Don't worry, folks, I said to them in my mind. I'll be out of your hair as quickly as possible.

"We have that dinner reservation," Cindy said, with a whining plea.

I was relieved when they finally all left me in the silence of the room. I opened my eyes and stared at the cop who came in and checked my handcuffs, then left.

I realized I was squeezing the pen in my right hand. I pushed myself up on the pillow and opened the notebook.

This shooting is a tragedy. All of us are desperate to understand. If you can shine any light on the answer . . . "

I squinted toward the notebook. "You want answers?" I whispered. "OK. Let's start at the beginning."

Words began to pour out on to the page. Words that seemed to be coming from some place beyond me, outside of my control.

HOME I wrote in big letters in the middle of my page, then drew a circle around the word with lines radiating out from it to other circles. Soon I was filling the circles:

FAMILY LOVE SECURITY RIGHTS.

An hour later I read my finished work and smiled.

BILL OF RIGHTS FOR CHILDREN

1. All children born in the U.S. have a God-given right to be nurtured the first eighteen years of life.

2. Children have the basic right to be embraced by love, security and support of family and church.

3. Children have the right to the carefree happiness of a childhood supervised by two responsible adults.

4. Children have the right to be treated with dignity in their school environment.

5. Children living in broken home situations have the right to demand their parents attend parenting classes before the child's anger leads to violence or self-destruction.

I held the notebook securely in my right hand. I wanted to scream for the lawyer. Wanted him to give my statement to the press. Wanted the president to sign it into law that very night.

XI

My Bill of Rights was taken as an admission of guilt and my personal journal, found near the river, was entered into evidence. Then, Drake's lies continued. He told the police he'd watched Jacob and me target practice with guns down on the river. Said we also took part in all kinds of occult ceremonies, planning the mass murder. He told them I was the one who carried the gun into the school that day. The liar said he'd heard us plan the shooting.

When the detectives asked why he didn't make some attempt to stop it, he stuttered and said, "I didn't think they were serious."

I wouldn't break my silence. It didn't seem worth it to me. Everything I loved was gone. Nothing I could say would make a difference. So for the next few months, I lived in a small cell, handcuffed, hobbling in ankle chains to and from the interrogation room where the detectives and my lawyer continued to bombard me with questions.

"Tokhe shni" I would tell them, looking straight into their eyes. I truly meant the words. "It doesn't matter."

The evening of the fifth day of the trial, I heard the rattle of keys in the cell door. I sat up on the cot and pulled the itchy, wool blanket up around my neck.

Ron Graves walked in and stood over me. He looked in disgust at the gray mass of beans uneaten on my food tray. "CJ, I'm afraid I have some bad news."

I stared at him and almost laughed. What news could he bring that would upset me in any way?

"Your dad is in the hospital. He's had a massive heart attack. It doesn't look real good, but he's getting the best care possible."

A shudder went through me as the words settled across my mind. When the lawyer went out and I sat alone in the darkness, I felt the wall of tears inside me rise like a great wave. The flood waters of grief hammered against the dam of self-control but it held.

That night, sitting on the corner of the cot with the blanket around me, I forced my mind into meditation. After a long struggle, I fell into a fitful sleep.

I was back in the cave. Jacob came to me. He brought me hot soup and dry clothes. He took warm oil, made me stretch out on a buffalo robe and began to soothe my aching muscles with massage.

"I love you, CJ." His voice was liquid with emotion and his green eyes sparked with passion.

"I love you, too," I said, touching his face. "I'm sorry I didn't say it before."

"We have to go back, you know. To Fremont."

Ron Graves was standing just outside the cell when I awoke. "As you know, they have your journal, CJ. It connects you to Jacob in an . . . incriminating way."

My face reddened. They had no right to read my personal journal. I'd tried to remember everything I'd written about Jacob. Would the tall detective share my most intimate thoughts with the world?

"I wish you would break your silence, CJ. If not for your sake, for the sake of your father's health. The sooner this is over, the better for him."

My eyes were swollen and blood shot as I sat beside the lawyer in the courtroom staring at Jacob's mother.

Mrs. Johnson walked to the stand. The way she pranced forward and flipped her head, I decided she was enjoying her day in the limelight. But just after she took the oath she seemed to collapse for no apparent reason. Her great mop of red hair flopped down as her head wilted into her hands. Sobs of anguish echoed throughout the court room and she began to tell the truth.

"Jacob was a good boy. He hated violence and alcohol and . . . Drake," she choked, trying to avoid the eyes of her husband. "Drake was mean to Jacob."

Everyone in the courtroom began to talk and the judge called for order. "Quiet, or I'll clear the room."

"What happened on the day of the shooting, Mrs. Johnson?" Ron Graves' voice echoed in the fresh silence.

"Drake was in a real bad mood that morning. He had a red-beer when he first got up, then he began to drink whiskey."

"She's lying!" Drake stood and started toward the front of the court room. The security guard grabbed him and Drake struggled until two other guards came from outside. Chairs tipped over and the lawyers had to jump to escape harm.

Drake was escorted out, screaming and swearing.

"Please," Ron Graves said, "continue."

"Drake was really drunk and when he got that way . . . he was mean to Jacob." Mrs. Johnson put her hand to her mouth to cover a sob.

"Do you need a brief recess?" Ron Graves asked.

Mrs. Johnson took her trembling hand from her face. "No. Jacob was leaving for school when Drake started in on him. He shoved him and . . . kicked him into the wall . . . " The color drained from Mrs. Johnson's face and she looked like one of those clowns, with rouge, red hair and a tragic stare.

"What were you doing while this took place, ma'am?"

Mrs. Johnson flinched and began to tremble. "Nothing. That's what I always did. Nothing."

Ron Graves stood patiently. "It's OK. Just continue when you can."

"Jacob left for school after that. It was late afternoon when we heard about . . . "

"Have you ever seen your son with the defendant, Connie Jean McGee?"

"No."

"To your knowledge, Jacob did not conspire with Connie Jean to stage the attack at Fremont High?"

"No. Drake told those lies to protect himself . . . because of the abuse."

"Objection, your honor. Hearsay." The district attorney was on his feet.

Chaos took over the court room. Mom and Mrs. Mac were near me, hugging me, while Ron Graves tried to get everyone to sit and the judge pounded his gavel.

"I'd like to call Connie Jean McGee to the stand." Ron looked down at me.

I rose slowly and started toward the front of the room. I put my hand on the Bible and swore to tell the truth. When I said, "I do," everyone in the courtroom gasped. The sound of my voice surprised even me.

My lawyer's eyes flashed with surprise and his face held a temporary expression of fear. He quickly regained his composure.

"CJ, would you please tell us what happened the day of the shooting?"

I cleared my throat and waited until the room was brittle with silence. "I was in study-hall when this scream came from the hallway. Run! Run! Then I heard shots. Kids began to explode out into the halls." The words that had been bottled up in me for months began to bubble out with a force all their own.

Ron Graves waited and the room remained silent.

"Someone . . . I think it was the substitute teacher, grabbed my hand and jerked me to my feet. She shoved me out the door and I became part of this stampede of kids that pushed through the big double doors out onto the lawn."

"At what point did you know who the shooter was?"

I swallowed and gripped the chair under me. "I was

standing outside. I heard one of the seniors sobbing to the sheriff. She said, "I don't think he goes to school at Fremont. I've never seen him before . . . but he's . . . shooting people. Shooting them. He came out of the gym and aimed his gun right at me, then turned and shot . . . the guy next to me . . . He had these feathers hanging from his hair and his face was painted."

The lawyer walked in front of me, pacing, his hands behind his back. "So you knew nothing about the shooting until that second."

"No."

"But you were friends with Jacob Johnson. Tell me about that."

"I was walking one afternoon along the Arkansas River south of our apartment and I saw Jacob sitting on the bank, alone. We became friends. We've been friends for many months."

"Did he ever show signs of violence or aggression toward the kids at school?"

"No. The boys picked on him constantly, but Jacob didn't fight back."

"Did he ever speak of getting even or say he wanted to kill them?"

"No."

"So you had absolutely no knowledge of what took place that day in the gym and hallway at Fremont High?"

"I still don't believe it."

Ron Graves gave me a quick smile. "No more questions, your honor."

The District Attorney took confident strides toward me

and his eyes gleamed with eagerness.

"So, Connie Jean, you're asking us to believe you are totally innocent in this? You admit you knew Jacob Johnson, spent months alone with him, yet you expect us to believe you are innocent?"

I gave the District Attorney a squinted stare, but remained quiet.

"You're going to sit and try to convince me that even though you were best friends with this boy, you had no hint that he was going to murder ten people? Why did you run then?"

"Your honor, he's badgering the defendant." Ron Graves was on his feet.

The judge warned the District Attorney, "Be careful, Mr. Ryan."

"No," I said, "I don't expect you to think that. I am guilty."

The courtroom erupted into a mass of outbursts. I heard my Mom's voice cry out above the crowd. "Do something, Ron."

The judge pounded his gavel and scowled. "One more time and you all go out. Please continue, young lady."

"We're all guilty," I said. "Society. Jacob's parents. The kids at school. But I'm the most guilty of all because . . . Jacob reached out to me and I let him down." I grabbed the smooth wood in front of me and gripped it, because the ground seemed to shake beneath me.

The old vibrating pain radiated across my shoulders and the iron hand clasped my throat. I gritted my teeth and prayed that the dam would hold back the flood of emotion that hammered, threatening to explode.

"Do you need a short recess?" The judge asked.

I shook my head. My mind leaped back to the day before the shooting. The scene I had blocked out of my mind until that moment. I understood then what my dreams had been telling me.

"The afternoon before the shooting." I began, Jacob and I were sitting cross-legged near the river, and Jacob began to stare at me with this narrow-eyed look in his green eyes.

"Are you my girl, CJ?" he asked, scooting close and taking my hand. "Belong?" The gesture so surprised me, I sat paralyzed for a moment, then pulled away from him. All I could think about was . . . " I looked straight at my mother and revealed the haunting secret. "All I could think about was that awful night in Wichita, my initiation into a gang called the Rebels. The tequila, the pot, the . . . rape."

My mother's jaw dropped and she stared in disbelief.

"Jacob's question rattled me so much, I got up and ran. He chased me."

"CJ, what is it?" he screamed. "What's wrong? Please don't go."

I had to swallow several times before I could continue because the memory of Jacob's last words . . . the last words he ever spoke to me, cut like a razor.

"The next day at school, I wrote him a note with all the horrid details of what had happened to me in Wichita. I planned to give it to him that night. We'd sit cross-legged and after he read it, he'd hold me gently and we'd cry together. Of all the boys on earth, Jacob would have understood my shame."

"I let him down," I said. "So I am guilty. I committed the worst crime of all. Jacob was in trouble. He didn't have anyone but me. He reached out and I turned away." My voice began to fade until the last words were a whisper. "Jacob Johnson was the only good thing I had in my life and I . . . killed him. In a way I killed them all."

XII

That afternoon I rode in silence with Mom back to our apartment. The dull pain from the trial, the reality of all that had happened pulled my spirits into a deep abyss.

Mom parked the car and reached for my hand. "Honey, we're home." She tried to put some enthusiasm into the words, but the effort ended in a depressing sigh.

My mother seemed to be struggling for words. "CJ, I'm so sorry for what you've been through. We'll do better . . . " Mom was trying. I felt bad for her. Nothing she could say now would heal what had been done.

"I need to go to Jacob's tee-pee," I said.

"You want company?" Mom asked.

I shook my head and started off alone.

As I neared Jacob's secret place along the river, I began to notice changes. Many feet had beaten a wide, deep path through what had once been dense brush. Most of the small trees were cut down and lay withered and brown along the path. I walked faster, panic seized me and I began to run.

Standing at the top of the hill looking toward the river, I stared. Jacob's tee-pee was gone. I stumbled to the spot where the hideout once stood, fell to my knees and tried to find at least a trace of his old campfire, but nothing remained. The tarp, every pole, even his fire ring of rocks, gone.

I stood and put my hands on the giant cottonwood, to assure myself that something remained of Jacob's world. I pulled my fingers back in horror. Freshly etched into the bark in crooked letters was the word, MONSTER.

Despair choked me. I fell to my knees, crawled to the edge of the river and vomited. Sitting, listening to the water I drifted into the shadows and thought, *I can't go on.*

I'm not sure how long I remained in the dark place, but finally I forced myself to breathe. It was as if Jacob were with me, breathing life into my lungs, saying "Inhale 1-2-3-4 exhale 1-2-3-4-5-6-7-8."

My mind began to journey back. I was in Wichita, it was after the rape and I'd missed my period. At first horrified, I kept thinking of the nasty, disgusting boy who had taken my virginity. The thought that his body fluid had created something in me spurred me to drink more, do more drugs.

Then one night, sitting with a joint, listening to the gang members plot a beating, I became disgusted with my life and yearned for something new. That's when the thought of my child germinated inside my mind.

The thought grew like the seed inside of me and each

day it brought new possibility. I started to think of how much better I could do than my parents had done. I'd be to my child what Pa Pa had been to me, a friend, a protector, a guide.

I was overcome, then, with a yearning to love my baby. I'd have someone who needed me, a reason to go on. I stopped drinking and smoking and began to take real good care of myself.

On a stormy Monday, I started having cramps in History class and excused myself. Crying at the heart-shaped confessions of love etched on the inside of the bathroom stall, I lost the life inside of me and the new hope that went with it.

It was then I got the tattoo. I cropped my shoulder-length hair into a buzz and dyed it purple. I felt dirty, battered and unnecessary. I wanted to die.

Dad loaded me into the car and took me to Pa Pa. On the drive he said, "Connie Jean, you are out of control."

So when Pa Pa saddled the horses and we rode down to the river, I knew he'd been given the dubious task of lecturing me.

We dismounted and I waited. Pa Pa stood looking at me for the longest time, then sighed. "Well, let's see it."

I smirked as I pulled my shirt off my shoulder revealing the tattoo.

A flash of amusement sparked in his old eyes. "Well, at least it's got something to do with ranching. Sort of."

I let my shirt slide back over my unicorn. "They can't make me do what they want anymore. I'm sick of them both."

"I know," he said, in his understanding way. "I know."

I was miserable and guilty. Pa Pa had lost Grammy just two months before and I could see the pain in his eyes, hear it in the weakening of his voice. Yet here he was, trying to help me.

I wanted to tell him about the gang, about the rape, the baby and how it had filled me with new hope. But none of it mattered any more, so I just said, "I hate my life, Pa Pa, I'm tired of it. I want to die."

With the speed of a snake, my grandfather grabbed my shoulders and shook me. He rattled me so hard my head snapped on my shoulders and I bit my tongue.

"Don't you ever, ever, ever, say that again!" He screamed the words, then jerked me up in his arms and held me in a vice-like grip. "Please, don't say that."

It was the first time Pa Pa had ever scolded me. He'd never lost patience with me in all of our years of friendship. His actions startled me so, it took several moments for me to respond.

"I'm sorry, Pa Pa. I'm just lost . . . I don't know which way to turn."

"Life has dark moments, CJ," Pa Pa said.

"Have you ever wanted to quit?" I asked.

The question seemed to sting him and he sat for a long time before he began to answer.

"I doubt your father's ever told you. He had a baby sister, Katherine." Pa Pa's struggle to tell the story was obvious in his eyes. "She was the most beautiful thing." He reached out his hand and ran it over my head, as if my strawberry curls hadn't changed into a purple butch. "Her hair was strawberry like yours and she had your deep green eyes that shone with energy."

I knew the story would end in sadness, and I didn't want it to. But it would, because it was such a great tragedy, my own father had never revealed a word to me.

"Katie loved horses from the day she could straddle one. She used to ride up in front of me when she was just a few months old. The first word out of her mouth was, 'orse.' When she took her first steps, she'd toddle down toward the corrals with your grandmother and me after her."

Pa Pa's eyes crinkled and he smiled. For a moment he seemed to take great pleasure in his memory.

"Oh, she'd howl like a coyote when one of us would carry her back to the house. Before she was five, she began to beg me to teach her to rope. On a bright afternoon in late September, Katie's fifth birthday, I promised her we'd begin roping lessons. We started together down toward the corrals. Katie ran ahead and crawled through the fence."

Pa Pa's fingers began to shake. When I reached out, he eagerly took my hands in his huge calloused paws. "The horses were feeding around the hay and Katie spooked them when she ran up."

My grandfather struggled with the next words and I knew, in that moment, he'd probably never told the story to anyone.

"The horses spooked . . . they ran different directions, kicking and twisting. Katie . . . one moment she was running toward them laughing, the next . . . she was on the ground. Quiet. Bleeding."

Pa Pa pulled away from me and leaned against a tree,

his voice echoed out across the creek and I stepped close so I could hear.

"My precious daughter had been kicked in the head. For the next six months she lay helpless in the hospital in a coma. Then she died. The day she left us, your grandmother and I came home. Things between us . . . weren't good. We blamed each other somehow for what happened and we couldn't talk."

Pa Pa stopped and his face twisted with uncertainty. Finally I touched his sleeve. "What happened?"

"That morning we came home and started the funeral arrangements, I lost my will to live. I took the shotgun from its peg on the gun rack, walked to the corral . . . where it had happened, and I put the gun to my head."

His words shocked me. "Pa Pa!"

"Your grandmother walked up behind me. 'James Alan McGee,' she said, 'don't you dare leave me! I need you. Alan needs you and your grandchildren will need you.' Her words shook me back to reality, and we cried together. Somehow we survived the next few years. We walked through the pain and did the best we could one long day at a time. Your dad grew up and married and moved away."

Pa Pa turned to me and lifted my chin. "Then one bright September day God sent us a gift. A little girl named Connie Jean after her aunt, Katherine Jean. She had the same strawberry curls and green eyes, the same love for the ponies."

I clung to my grandfather and all I could think of was how empty my entire life would have been if I'd never had Pa Pa in it.

"You can't quit, CJ. You're part of a wonderful, joyous, painful circle of mystery, you see, You must follow that and see where it leads you."

I snapped back into the present and sat listening to the river. I knew Pa Pa was right. I couldn't quit. I had no idea what was next and life seemed overwhelmingly sad, but Pa Pa's memory gave me the strength to stand and start walking. When I reached the top of the hill, I had an almost irresistible urge to turn and look back. But I couldn't.

The thought of losing Jacob, Prophet, and Vision was too much to embrace at that moment.

Dad drove from Dallas that afternoon. I hadn't seen him for days. The courthouse had been off limits because of his health.

When he came to the door, he looked thin and pale. I went into his arms and we held each other in silence for a moment.

"Are we ready?" he said to Mom.

Mom nodded her head in agreement.

I stared at first one, then the other. Dad had called on his cell phone and asked if I'd go for a drive with him for the afternoon. I had no idea Mom was coming. My first reaction was dread. I'd looked forward to a peaceful time with Dad and I had little desire to sit between them for even ten minutes.

As Dad drove, I studied his face and for the first time noticed the deep lines and how gray his hair was near the temples. I thought about the baby sister he'd lost, about his pain and wondered if someday he'd talk to me about it.

"Are they saying that you'll be back to 100%? "

Dad took my hand. "I'll never be the same, Connie Jean. But the heart attack is only partly responsible for the changes I'm about to make."

"Changes?"

"That morning when I first read your Bill of Rights, I broke down and wept. When they took you off to jail, I started to understand what you'd been through because of my mistakes. I began to change before the heart attack."

I watched Dad and listened as he drove. "What change?" I asked again. I looked at Mom, wondering why she was being so quiet.

"CJ, I agree with you about a lot of things. Your life would have been much better if I'd stayed with your mother, worked on my marriage and avoided divorce. You were robbed of the best part of your childhood because of my selfishness."

"Tokhe shni," I said. "It's something Jacob used to say. 'It doesn't matter.'

"Yes, it does matter. I was selfish and too busy wanting my life to be great and I didn't give your happiness one thought. So . . . I'm going to try to make up for that."

He pulled the car over to the old store on the gravel road that led to my grandparents' homestead. I looked out and realized where we were.

Dad smiled. "Could I interest you ladies in a cup of cider?"

Mom took my hand as we started into the country store. The old man behind the counter gave a toothless grin when he saw me come in the door with my parents. Dad ordered three ciders. The man filled the cups and handed them over.

"You made yourself quite a trip, little gal. I knowed that day you come in here, you was hungry and scared. I didn't call the cops. No sir. Wadn't none of my business so I just kept my nose out of it. Besides, I remembered you from comin in here with your daddy. You always seemed like a good kid to me."

"Thanks, Mr. Bartlet," Dad said, placing three dollars on the counter.

"Yes, sir, thanks," I said.

In the car, I watched the familiar landscape coming up in front of us as we drove. I thought about where Vision swam the river and tried to guess from the highway where we were when the cops finally caught us.

The scene of my pony being shot from under me made the familiar iron clamp of pain settle around my throat. I wanted to ask about Vision and Prophet. I'd wanted to ask many times, throughout the trial and since my release, but each time I lost my nerve. Maybe I still wasn't ready to know.

"CJ, I'm proud of you for running away. For taking a stand." Dad said. "I hope you'll forgive me, but I also read your journal. The one you had with you on your trip." He reached in the back seat and handed me the notebook.

I held it in my lap, staring. It was spotted with rain drops, splashed with mud, and curled at the edges.

Then, Dad placed my cedar box in my hands. "The fishermen who spotted you on the river returned all of your things to the police."

159

I smoothed my hands over the picture of the river painted on the box and my fingers trembled.

"You loved him, I know," Mom said, squeezing my hand. "I can only imagine how much it hurts . . . what happened at Fremont, the shock." She pulled a tissue from a box on the floor and fingered it. "CJ, I'm so sorry about what happened to you in Wichita. Sorry I was so wrapped up in . . . myself that I didn't take time to . . . " Mom's words faded into silence.

We were pulling up into the old gravel drive that led to my grandparents' place. I looked through the side window and a thousand memories of Grammy and Pa Pa flooded over me. "I miss them," I said. "Every day."

"Would it help to be closer to your grandparents?" Dad looked at me, smiling. He stopped the car and pointed out into the grassy field in front of us.

I blinked my eyes and stared. It was Vision! Standing, grazing, knee deep in blue stem grass. I crawled over Mom, hit the car door and started running. Just as Vision saw me and lifted his head, I heard a familiar bark and turned. Prophet ran toward me, yelping each time a foot hit the ground. He bolted into my arms with a jump and licked me all over my neck, whining.

My gelding nickered and stepped forward, wanting in on the reunion.

"Wish I had a camera," Dad said, walking up. He knelt right down in the deep grass as I nuzzled Vision and kissed Prophet over and over on the nose.

"But . . . I don't understand. They shot Vision . . . I thought . . . "

"It was a tranquilizer, Connie Jean. I didn't know until your Mom told me about Mrs. Mac getting Prophet out of the animal shelter. I did some checking. They were holding your horse too. I had someone pick them up yesterday.

"Why did you bring them here?"

"CJ, your mother and I have done a lot of talking these past few weeks. We finally stopped blaming long enough to take responsibility for our mistakes, get honest with each other. We think its time for you to have a little happiness. We've both had our stab at it."

I looked at my dad. I couldn't remember him ever calling me CJ. I looked at Mom, who remained quiet. "What?"

"Tomorrow, I'm having a double wide trailer pulled in and set up over there, beneath the trees next to the old house," Dad said. "I've quit my job in Dallas. I'm coming out here to build a log house, right in that very spot where the old homestead stands. You can live here with me and attend school in Fairfax, if you want."

"Well, I think . . . " Mom started in her old hateful tone, but stopped herself with an obvious effort. "Whatever you want, honey. Mrs. Mac and I might even make it out to go fishing." Mom said.

"You? Fishing?" I asked. I smiled and an old familiar feeling beckoned from somewhere in the past. It teased me with fond thoughts of family and home.

Dad knelt and petted Prophet, then stood and walked toward Vision.

"But Dad, what about Cindy? Will she live with us?"

My father's face turned ashen. "Cindy isn't with me any more. The . . . heart attack, all the recovery period."

"I'm so sorry, Dad."

"Your grandfather tried to tell me that you were the most important thing in my life." Dad ran his hand through Vision's white mane. "I hope he knows I've finally listened."

While Vision's velvet lips tickled across my hair and Prophet nuzzled my neck, I remembered my conversation with Pa Pa about the divorce. "Can't you tell them, Pa Pa? Can't you tell them I'm important?"

Then I thought of my journey and how my grandfather visited me in the circle of light, "You will make it home, CJ." That very morning Pa Pa's memory had helped me cling to life.

"He knows," I said, standing, with Prophet held close. "Pa Pa knows."

The reality of what was happening began to slowly filter through my mind, like autumn leaves gently falling, floating on the wind. Life could be better now. Easy. I could leave the nightmare of Fremont behind. Live in peace along the river on the old home place with Vision and Prophet near.

But all of those wonderful thoughts left me cold. I thought about my old childhood home in Texas, of the nightmare in Wichita, of Jacob's tee-pee. I no longer knew where I belonged or if I belonged anywhere.

"Keeeer, Keeeer, Keeeer." The cry came to my ears like the distant beat of an Indian drum breaking the silence of the night, bringing peace to the turmoil in my soul.

I stared up into the clear morning sky. The red-tail dived through the clouds, drifted south and east, toward Tulsa, then faded out of sight.

"I have to go back to Mom's, to the apartment for now."
The words came from somewhere outside of my control as
I stared at the sky. Jacob's words echoed in my mind. "We
have to go back, you know. To Fremont."

"Sweetheart, are you OK?" Dad touched my shoulder.

"That may be real tough, honey," Mom said. "Your
entire life has been in the papers. All the kids will know
about you and Jacob, your running away, the trial." Mom
was actually looking at me. Waiting. Willing to listen.

"It won't be easy," I said. "But who am I to take the easy
way out? For five years I've condemned you and Dad for
getting a divorce instead of working on your marriage."

Mom and Dad exchanged a look that made me know
they'd never place blame on each other again.

Dad's eyes shone with pride and he grinned. "I admire
your courage," he said. "And I'll be here. I'll come get you
every week-end if you want."

I nodded. "I'd like that." I walked back to my pony and
began to run my hands over his back, down his withers, to
his flank.

"I happen to have your saddle and bridle in the trunk,"
Dad said, "if you're interested?"

Vision was anxious to run. I allowed him to have a free
rein and the wind felt good against my face. I rode to Pa
Pa's favorite spot on the creek beneath a stand of giant cottonwoods.

When I dismounted and stood remembering, Vision
nudged me with his nose. Prophet scratched my leg with
his paw. The great wall of grief hammered against the dam

of resistance and a sob erupted in the form of a name.

"Jacob, Jacob, Jacob."

Vision stepped toward me, offering his strong shoulder and I threw my arms around him just as the dam broke. Jagged pieces of grief rattled out, like great chunks of concrete crumbling, crumbling. My shoulders shook and I clung to my pony, hoping that if I didn't survive the flood, the gods would deliver me to the spirit world with my pony and dog.

Sobs of disbelief, of sorrow, of regret, gushed from the deepest canyons of my soul. I cried for Jacob and for his pain, for the kids who'd lost their lives, for their parents and all of their loved ones. So many people hurt. Jacob's pain mutiplied into more pain.

"I love you, Jacob. I am your girl. I always will be."

When my body finally quieted and tears would no longer come, I walked to the creek and splashed cool water on my face. I sat for a long time holding Prophet in my lap.

I knew I couldn't change what had happened. No amount of grief or regret would turn back time. I also knew my life would forever be linked to Jacob, to his tenderness and his pain. Somehow I had to find a way to bring honor to his memory by helping the people he had hurt.

Mom and Dad were sitting at the old, splintery picnic table talking when I rode up and unsaddled Vision.

When Dad opened the car door for me, Prophet dived into the front seat. He barked an invitation to the rest of us.

I looked at Mom. Dad looked at Mom.

"What the heck," she said, "if we get kicked out of the apartment, we'll move or buy a house or something."

"I know a realtor," Dad said. "She's a workaholic, but a great realtor."

Mom and Dad laughed together as we settled in the car and Prophet burrowed into my lap. The cry of the red-tail came faintly to my ears through the open window as we drove down the gravel road.

"Keeeeer, Keeeeer, Keeeeer."

Prophet put his nose against my neck and I held him as Jacob's words echoed in my mind.

"I will call him Prophet. He will lead the People to see with the eyes in their hearts."

My mom and dad divorced when I was seven. Mama left our home. Dad remarried several years later and we moved away from the farm I dearly loved. In the aftermath of our broken family, I was thrown into a quagmire of alcoholics, violence, court custody battles and stepparents.

In 1960, when I was twelve years old, I ran away. On a brilliant autumn afternoon, I saddled my pony and began a journey from Purcell, Oklahoma back toward Ponca City and the only 'home' I'd ever known. For the next three days, I hid with my dog and horse among the cottonwood trees along the Canadian River while the police chased me.

I understand the pain and confusion that comes with a broken family. I remember the constant yearning to belong. For many years, I tried to cover that pain in destructive ways. It does not help.

Please do not choose violence toward yourself or others. Nurture yourself with love and honor and reach out to others in need so that you will learn to 'belong' to your best self.

And remember . . . I love you, no matter what.

-The Author-